NEPHILIM

THE AWAKENING

(Book 2 of the Nephilim Series)

Written by

Kirk Allen Kreitzer

Published by Kreitzer Publishing

ISBN: 978-0-9917922-0-7

Cover by: Steven Kalcsits

www.nephilimtheremembering.com

From the Author:

I am very excited to finally release Nephilim The Awakening. I believe you will find it a much faster and darker read then The Remembering. I want to thank my family and friends who encouraged me to keep Curtis, Eavery and the gang going and a special thanks to Becky Seguin for her advice and ideas and for reading yet *another* rough draft. I want to give very special thanks to Deb Nissen, for her very keen eye and natural editing skills and to Steven Kalcsits for designing the cover and for basically putting up with me.

And of course, thanks to my wife Lisa and my daughter Alexsys for supporting me and my hobby over the last two years.

I dedicate this book to my brother Arthur and my father Donald.

A bit of the last chapter from NEPHILIM the remembering:

"What am I going to do? What are we going to do?" Curtis asked, feeling the true weight of his situation pull on him. The idea of someone going out of their way to hurt or kill Charlie filled his mind with unwanted and indescribable images. Deep inside, his self-control was slipping to the point of panic. Not to mention the fact that the world has changed and Vivica was still unaware of any of it.

"Right now they don't know you," Eavery said, trying to sow some calm into Curtis.

"But they will!" Curtis blurted his chest tight. "You know, in the military we are trained to face and fight the enemy. But when the enemy can be anyone — your grocer, your cab driver, your friggin' neighbour — and they're targeting your family, how can you fight that? Where do you make your stand?"

"Well, the first thing, Curtis, is training," Eavery said, trying to put Curtis at ease. "Remember that feeling you got before the van hit you? How you practically froze time and moved out of the way? That is only part of your abilities."

That makes sense, Curtis thought to himself. He put the cup of cold coffee down and stood up straight, still amazed how good he felt. Yeah, training!

"If they don't know me yet, at least I have that up on them. So training; how do we do that?"

Eavery wasn't sure; in fact, he was stalled on that issue. He lowered his eyes, "I don't know."

Curtis stared blankly at Eavery. He could feel the bubbling of panic again.

"Wow, you're a lot of help. How have you managed? What have you been doing all these years?"

"Me?" Eavery paused with some self-reflection. "I move around a lot, but I'm not really on the KRÁJCÁR radar."

Curtis watched Eavery become uncomfortable, his posture sinking, as if he was trying to hide himself in plain sight.

"You're not? Why? How have you managed that?" Curtis felt some hope fill in a little of the hole that the stress was creating. Again, Curtis watched Eavery awkwardly search for his words.

"They are not as interested in my heritage as much as yours. But, perhaps you could talk to Jophiel; maybe there is something he can do?"

Curtis watched Eavery with suspicion for a few seconds and then guilt mixed itself in with the tumultuous cocktail of emotions. The stress is causing me to question the very nature of my friend, he thought to himself.

"Jophiel!" Curtis said aloud triumphantly, as if solving some great equation. "Do you think he would help?"

"I don't know!"

Curtis felt the rapidly eroding foundation beneath his feet solidify just a little.

“Have the Cherubim helped a lot of people in the past?” he asked, hoping for some positive news.

“Not that I am aware of,” Eavery garbled, running his fingers over his mouth at the same time.

A little more foundation eroded.

Curtis felt the tingle of electricity in the air. Then the hair on the back of his neck straightened, reminding him that he needed a hair cut before he went back to work. Then he watched the hair on his arms rise. A curious look popped onto Eavery’s face and both of them looked around the kitchen. A second later, the now familiar sound of discharging electricity filled the house. Fingers of platinum-coloured plasma arced along the floor, across the cupboards and counter top, up the stove and along the door of the fridge. Pictures and drawings Charlie coloured at daycare fell to the floor as the current neutralized the cheap magnets that held them to the appliances. Finally, there was a thunderous crack, a flash of white light, and the distinct smell of ozone.

Curtis and Eavery stood motionless, waiting for someone to appear. Then the black Cherubim with the silver ribbons swirling beneath his skin entered the kitchen from the living room, behind Eavery. Still standing modestly tall with his wings folded behind his back, Jophiel approached them. Where the satchel and scroll once sat on his left hip there was now a gleaming golden scabbard and sword. As he entered the kitchen, he had to duck his head and twist his back to fit himself through the doorframe. Eavery stepped to the side to give the angelic being more room.

Standing in front of the two men, Jophiel looked down directly at Curtis, stared into him, read him, every fiber, and every thought.

The silver ribbons under the Cherubim's skin began to mix and swirl faster, more energized, almost chaotic.

Jophiel placed his left hand on top of the handle of his sword, glanced over at Eavery and then slowly back at Curtis.

"I'll do it."

NEPHILIM the awakening

CHAPTER TWENTY-ONE

"You will?" Curtis and Eavery said together in unified disbelief.

Jophiel, internally amused by the shocked response, held his stoic posture. "Yes. Actions that are still unclear to us at the moment have been set into play. What we do know is the outcome could completely change this world – your world, and ours. And you, Curtis Papp, are somehow inexplicably linked."

Curtis side looked at Eavery and back again to Jophiel. He didn't know what cosmic shift was about to take place, or how he could possibly be mixed up with it, but he felt the cold breath of guilt and judgment pass over him. He found himself uncertain on how to respond to the accusation.

"Is it because of the KRÁJCÁR?" Curtis guessed. It wasn't a solid guess but what else was there?

"No," Jophiel said, then shifted slightly trying to stand his full height in the small kitchen. "The KRÁJCÁR play a different role in the Celestial realm." Jophiel turned his gaze over to Eavery. "Perhaps your friend here has heard something?"

Curtis, a little surprised, turned to Eavery. Having both sets of eyes staring and waiting, Eavery instantly felt the pressure of being cornered.

"Umm... no, we haven't heard of anything either."

Curtis watched Eavery squirm uncomfortably under the spotlight.

"Oh!" Jophiel continued to hold his stare. "I was under the impression that your intervention with Curtis had more to do with stratagem and planning than serendipity."

Curtis watched Jophiel and Eavery lock eyes. As Jophiel's silver swirls beneath his flawless black skin twirled and mixed excitedly, Curtis noticed his wife's philodendron that was hanging in the kitchen window begin to grow madly out of control.

"Perhaps omnipotence dwindles with age," the Cherubim goaded.

"For once we know as little as you, Jophiel. And what a disappointing feeling this is. Now I understand why you are always so aggressive," Eavery countered, no longer sheepish and uncomfortable but standing tall.

"What the hell are you guys talking about?" Curtis broke in, trying to diffuse a tense situation; it looked like a throw-down was about to erupt in his kitchen.

"Your training," Jophiel said as he casually turned his head back to Curtis, "we will start right now."

Jophiel stepped back into the dining room where he felt a little less confined. Curtis, caught off guard by Jophiel's abrupt change of topic, stumbled out a meekly, "Okay!" Then looked over to Eavery who was still visibly tense.

Standing majestic again, Jophiel began, "You have already seen your ability to slow time; it is a talent that you must master – it is indispensable during combat."

Curtis thought back to the incident on the sidewalk in front of Alderney Landing when a white van almost ran into him and his four year old daughter, Charlie. He remembered how he had slowed the world down and was able to leap out of the way of the speeding vehicle (for the most part). Unfortunately his new friend, Brent Martin, wasn't so lucky.

“Practice this every day,” Jophiel lectured, returning Curtis back to the conversation. “A good training tool is the faucet at your sink. Turn it on so you get a steady stream of water, and with your mind slow it down and pass your finger in between the individual drops. After you have mastered that, walk around outside during the next rain storm and work your way in between the falling rain.”

As Jophiel mentioned examples, Curtis felt his mind wanting to practice right then and there. On the far side of the room, Sphinx, the Papp’s black and white house cat, dressed up as a ballerina in a flattering pink Barbie tutu and a sequined, pink brazier, shamefully sauntered in through the doorway. Curtis focused and slowed the cat’s walk. Surprisingly, Jophiel continued at the same speed.

“Good!” Jophiel commented.

“Why haven’t you slowed down?” Curtis asked.

“That only works on lesser beings,” he replied and then nodded at Eavery, who was also moving his head and eyes very slowly as he turned towards Curtis in slow motion. Then Eavery flashed him a quick wink and a large Cheshire cat grin. Eavery laughed out loud as if he had just told the world’s funniest joke.

Curtis laughed with him and the world snapped back to its natural pace.

“Another attribute of yours,” Jophiel said as he carried on with the training, “is extending your energy, or divine field, in a particular direction at a specific object.” Jophiel gracefully extended his right arm and opened his fingers. A plastic apple from a glass bowl of plastic fruit on the dining table seamlessly lifted up and drifted over to the angel until it gently rested in his palm.

“That? I can do that? I can move things with my mind – fuck yeah!” Curtis said excitedly, and then paused, cautiously looking around for the young ears of his daughter, his eyes beaming as his imagination played with the awesome potential of his gift.

"You have this ability, Curtis, but it will be up to you to train yourself to do it. Remember our conversation about energy? Your divine field is yours to manipulate how you need it." Jophiel brought the apple to his mouth.

"Wait – it's plastic," Curtis said trying to warn him. Instead of the startled expression of a Cherubim with a collapsed plastic apple in his mouth, Curtis watched disappointedly as Jophiel bit into fresh fruit.

"Wow!" Curtis said amazed. Eavery stood beside him twirling his finger in the air un-amused and bored, sulking at his still wounded pride.

"Will I be able to do that?" Curtis asked in amazement, "Generate real food like that?"

"No!" Jophiel chortled and took another bite of the juicy apple, leaving his reply to hang in the air.

"Now, look at an object," he garbled with a mouth full of fruit. "Look at the green pear in the bowl. If it helps you to focus, stretch out your arm."

Curtis did as he suggested.
"Now use the linear extension of your arm to stretch and broadcast yourself to the pear."

Like a child at Christmas, the smile on Curtis's face shone with excitement. He could feel the energy inside him vibrate. Eavery watched Curtis; his excitement also grew for his friend. This was pretty amazing stuff for a human to be accomplishing.

In Curtis's mind, he felt he was on the brink of becoming a comic book hero, a real life X-MAN. He extended his fingers and felt the energy field build up on their tips. Then he willed the energy out, projecting it.

They all watched as the glass bowl with the plastic fruit launched off the table, smashed into the wall, and finally shattered on the dining room's hardwood floor. The loud crash sent Sphinx scrambling out of the room. Both Curtis's and Eavery's mouth dropped in astonishment.

"Did you see that?" Curtis hollered out loud to everyone and back handed Eavery on the shoulder.

"Not bad for a first try," Jophiel said, nodding his head in approval, "but you'll have to work on that."

The patter of little feet approached from behind as Charlie, always the inquisitor, came in through the kitchen.

"What happened? Did someone drop something? Mommy doesn't like it when people play around the table. Boy, you're big!" she said all in one breath as she looked up at the angel. "You've got wings! Just like my Pegasus Pony."

"Charlie!" Curtis blurted with embarrassment. Eavery snickered. The four year old looked up at her dad with a "What?" on her face.

Jophiel turned his attention to the young Papp, lightly amused by her candid tongue.

"You are interesting – for such a little human." Jophiel studied her some more. "You are different than your father. You hold my blood line, yes, but there is more to you. Much more."

Curtis looked down at Charlie, squinting. He still couldn't see anything about her that stood out beyond the appearance of an average four-year-old girl. What do they see?

Charlie looked at all three pairs of eyes in turn and then down at the broken glass bowl and plastic fruit spread across the floor.

"I'm not going to tell mommy someone broke her bowl. It will be our little secret," she whispered to her father. Then, without saying another word, she turned around and left back through the kitchen, leaving the three of them once again to themselves.

Curtis gave a quick glance first to Jophiel and then to Eavery. A smile crept across Eavery's face; he was charmed by the little one's character.

Back to business Jophiel continued where he left off. "These two new abilities will be most beneficial during combat. But there is more. Your near future holds something immense. I am afraid I cannot see it, and because of that, I fear it will be something terrible. Your new skills will help you, but you will need a weapon."

Placing his right hand on his sword, he wrapped his mighty fingers around the white celestial marble handle with carved finger channels. As he pulled it straight out he unsheathed the magnificent golden blade. Imprinted angelic script ran down both sides of the blade: Out of Many Came One. Both Curtis's and Eavery's eyes widened in admiration. Eavery's face held a look mixed with both excitement and suspicion.

"The angelic celestial sword is constructed from the yielder's own soul; it is an intimate part of the yielder, a part of me," Jophiel lectured, swaying the sword in front of him as if it was on display at an auction. "These weapons were created out of necessity when the angelic realm was divided. When Ha-Sata created his own army, we needed weapons to defeat them."

Curtis couldn't take his eyes off the sword. Its radiance almost glowed. And as large and incredibly heavy as it looked, it seemed to float on the air.

Jophiel continued, "Only the sword's creator, the one who shares the bond with the sword, can wield it. No other angel or demon can use it – especially against the originator – if they happened to take it from him. And no human would be able to lift it off the ground, if by chance he was to come across one."

“So – are you going to show me how to create one of my own?” Curtis inquired, gobsmacked by the beauty and power emanating from the sword.

Jophiel stared at his sword and his black reflection mirrored on the blade. He remembered countless battles they shared together and the countless demons and tainted angels’ lives they had ended together. He remembered the thousands of times it had saved his life. The bond he shared with his sword, the same bond shared by all angels and their swords, was equivalent to the symbiotic relationship one shares with his own hand, or the nose on his face.

“No Curtis.” Jophiel grabbed the bladed end with his left hand and held the handle out to Curtis. “You must have this one.”

CHAPTER TWENTY-TWO

Sudbury, Ontario

"Where are we going now?" Jake Rogus said as he stood at his bathroom sink and washed the remaining blood from under his cuticles.

"There are places to go," replied the **darkness**. The voice filled Jake's head like an air traffic controller guiding a pilot through the cockpit headset. Only a control tower can't physically take control of the pilot the way the **darkness** could when it feels like taking control of Jake.

"We're not done! You said we'll make them pay," Jake protested.

"We've killed your boss with his own keyboard and mouse while he was sitting at his desk, and you just watched as all the blood in your ex-whore's body spilled across the kitchen floor as you slit her throat. What more do you want, puppet?" the **darkness** said, annoyance heavy in its tone.

"We didn't kill the kid. I want the fucker dead."

"I believe I have unleashed a sociopath unto this world," the **darkness** mocked.

"I appreciate your ambitions, but a massive murdering spree is going to get you caught. And... I can't touch that infant."

"What?" Jake said out loud looking into the mirror. "Why?" Jake demanded.

"Because it is innocent," the **darkness** returned Jake's eyes back down so they could focus on cleaning the blood from under his (the puppet's) finger nails. "It can see me. I can't tempt it."

Jake dragged his eyes back to the mirror to look into their face.

“Demons devour babies whole all the time.”

“No, that is merely propaganda created by religions to scare children. But Man, on the other hand, kill children all of the time. That’s what they like about you.”

“They? Who ‘they’?”

“By the Infernal Deities – the demons you were talking about,” the **darkness** said, annoyed.

“Fine, fine, but the brat is sleeping right there in the crib; I can kill it on the way out,” Jake said impatiently. A single-minded focus of hate cluttered his half of his brain, making him anxious.

“Ahhhhhhhh!” Jake screamed in agony and dropped to his knees, clenching his chest as the **darkness** gripped Jake’s heart and squeezed it from within.

“I grow tired of your arguing, puppet, along with your constant talking. Your head is filled with senseless drivel and it clouds your direction.”

Jake fell to his side on the bathroom floor. Spittle foamed at the corner of his mouth. The crushing pain in his chest prevented him from inhaling or exhaling as flashes of light blinked in and out of his vision.

“Consider it a universal understanding,” the **darkness** continued, unaffected by the physical stress he was placing on his human marionette. “It was declared before your species even existed. The innocent is not to be touched. And it so happens, human infants fall beneath that ambiguous diktat. I do believe An, who you know as God, did that on purpose – c'est la vie.”

Returning his attention back to the miscreant, the **darkness** released his grip on Jake’s heart just moments before it would have ended his life. Jake could feel the nourishing blood circulating again through his body as his heart ached but began to pump. Finally, he inhaled sharply, coughing and choking as he drew in the saliva and mucous that had pooled in his airway.

“We’ll just wait a couple of years, Jakey, as the world corrupts your little souvenir from your ‘one-night-stand.’ Then we’ll come back. Does that suit you?” the **darkness** said, its tone resembling that of a parent speaking to a toddler.

“Now get up and start packing; we’ve got to leave. Your neighbours surely heard your pathetic screaming.”

Jake Rogus pushed himself onto his knees. Clutching his chest with his right hand, he wiped the string of drool from his lips with his left.

“Where are we going?” Jake whispered, both from the pain in his throat and fearing another display of authority.

“Somewhere in this world, I sense my brother. We have some unfinished business.”

Jake pulled himself up by the edge of the sink and stood on weak, shaky legs as he looked into the mirror. His contorted face still reflected the painful ordeal he had endured just seconds earlier.

“And don’t ever,” Jake’s mouth involuntarily spoke aloud, “refer to me as a fucking demon again. Or I will show you what real pain is.”

CHAPTER TWENTY-THREE

Veszprém, Hungary
Bishop's Palace

Gergõ Mátyás leaned back in his chair as the head of the Group of Seven and of the Társadalom, which is the KRÁJCÁR's executive committee. He spread his arms out and caressed his fingers across the 14th century English oak table feeling the scratches and indentations in its lacquered surface. "So, Elek, why did you call us all together-again? We just had a meeting last Monday."

Elek Szalai was the Társadalom's vice chair and member of the Group of Seven. He stood at the bar in his black, striped Armani suit with his back to the other six members sitting at the table; he knew they were eyeing him and less than patiently waiting for an explanation. The Társadalom had a meeting once a month, but the Group of Seven only sat together three times a year – and each member lived in a different city throughout Europe. Any additional meetings were very rare, and twice in the same week had never been done before in its sixteen hundred year history.

Elek poured himself a few ounces of the rare 1937 Glenfiddich Scotch Whiskey from the crystal decanter and then reseated the topper. Pressing his position longer, he sipped the whiskey and allowed the bitter mossy-oak taste to seize his tongue. He turned and sauntered over to his place at the table.

Elek reached into the front pocket of his suit coat and pulled out a folded piece of charred paper. He tossed it in front of József Söröss.

Gergõ leaned forward and eyed the paper and then looked back to Elek. "Enough with the drama, Elek, what's on the paper?"

József quickly unfolded the paper; burnt edges encompassed three of its sides. Gáspár Török, seated next to him and across from Elek, leaned over. “Are we to presume you think this is authentic?”

“Oh, it is authentic,” Elek replied smugly, taking another sip.

“You got us all back here for this... this scribble? My daughter’s wedding is tomorrow and I need to fly back to Rome tonight,” József said, tossing the paper back onto the table.

Gergõ eyed each man individually, watching as their faces broadcast their frustration at the unprecedented breach of protocol. In turn, each head swiveled back at Gergõ, waiting for a satisfying chastisement and rapid dismissal of the meeting. They knew Elek needed it. His age and prominence in the Társadalom had always made him the first to criticize Gergõ’s decisions and direction. Elek’s personal belief that the KRÁJCÁR should be led by the two of them, equally, had even caused a small division of allegiance within the Society. This created more than a minor annoyance for Gergõ when several of his plans were squashed due to a large number of “nay” votes from the Társadalom membership.

Gergõ leaned forward again and retrieved the piece of paper.

Reading it, Gergõ turned his gaze up to Elek who was still standing behind his chair. “Where did you find this?”

“One of the Testvériség priests retrieved it in northern Chile after he finished his assignment.”

“Gergõ, you don’t actually believe it is real?” Gáspár said in disbelief.

“Is there more?” Gergõ asked, disregarding Gáspár’s question.

“No. After the brother finished the assignment he set the house ablaze. Drifting on the wind was this little piece of paper still on fire. It landed on his lap, literally.”

Sliding the paper back down the table so the group could get another look, Gergõ leaned back in his chair and looked up at the large shield of the KRÁJCÁR crest up on the wall.

"It looks Phoenician," Henrik Koscis said from the far end of the table.

"It's not Phoenician," Elek said matter-of-factly as he watched the evidence and its consequence solidify into Gergõ's mind.

"It's Brâmhi," another suggested.

"It's pre-Brâmhi," Elek returned flatly.

"It is Hebrew. It is definitely Hebrew," József said strongly and with authority. "You see that first letter, that's the letter 'Pe.' It's a little messy; whoever wrote it was sloppy..."

"It is fucking pre-Hebrew. It's prewritten history, it is the language that all written language originally came from. That is why it looks a little like each of them."

Gergõ had had enough. "Angelic Script? Is that what you are getting at Elek? That someone was actually writing on paper the written language used by angels?"

Elek finished his Glenfiddich and placed the glass down on the table. The five other men all leaned forward in their chairs, watching his every move.

"This wasn't printed off from some website Gergõ. It was found at the residence of an assignment. Who could say how much more was written there? If this Antonio Gomez could write these few letters, then he could write more. He could write a book, or two. If he could read it, then eventually he would be able to speak it."

Elek looked around to the other men. Shock and terror stained their faces.

"And when you can do both, you have the Knowledge. Divine knowledge. The language with which Yahweh speaks to his Elohim. The exact words He used during the Creation. The words He used to cast Ha-Sata out of Paradise."

"Or to return him," József said under his breath.

Gergõ ran his hands up and around his elongated skull, a habit of his when he got stressed and sought enlightenment from his ancestors.

"You knew that was Angelic Script this whole time and you had it folded up just sitting in your pocket?" Károly Németh, the seventh and final member said in disgust. "That is sacrilege. Those three letters make that piece of paper the most holy relic on the planet. It needs to be placed in a chamber of inert gas behind bullet proof glass."

"No, it needs to be burned!" Gergõ interjected. Gasps of disbelief and argument spilled from the men, except from Elek. It was his turn to watch Gergõ, curious about where he was going with this.

Gergõ continued. "We'll send a team over to cleanse the small village and anyone suspected of knowing this... Gomez."

"What?" Elek shouted. "Are you insane, Gergõ? We have here written proof that the real Angelic Script is out there. There is probably a very good chance that another Nephilim is living in that village who also has copies of the script, who may also be able to read it and translate it."

"That is why we need to eliminate them. Have you forgotten it is our purpose to prevent the Divine Knowledge from spreading into the corrupted minds of men? This is the exact reason why the angel Carviel charged the prophet Attila with his sacred duty. This is why he was given the Isten Kardja, the Sword of God, knighting him the Scourge of God. This is the reason he created the KRÁJCÁR, why we have the Társadalom, the Testvériség. This is the reason, Elek, why we even exist. To think otherwise is too spit on Lord Attila's grave."

Elek sprang to his feet. "Gergõ, stop and think for a second. We have men associated in every government within the G20. We have our men in both Israel and in the Arab league. Now is the time to unite the world under one hand – our hand. Divine providence has led us to the script. The Knowledge, gentlemen would give us the world. One government. One country." Elek smiled, his eyes alight with the thought of power.

Gergõ stood up and slammed his fist into the ancient oak. "That is blasphemy! The KRÁJCÁR was created to prevent the corruptible wills of man from wielding the power of the Divine Knowledge. Attila brought down Rome with that mandate and we have been suppressing similar ambitions ever since. No, we are going to send a team in there to wipe out all existence of those letters. That's final!"

The two men stood glaring at each other, neither one taking his seat.

"The Mátyás family has held solely onto the Vezető chair for far too long. Every member here knows that when the prophet Attila created the KRÁJCÁR, he designed it so the Vezető would be shared by two families: the Mátyás and the Szalai."

"That is true," Henrik confirmed, nodding his head. Everyone else at the table was stunned into silence at the turn of events.

József shook his head in frustration. "Elek, do we have to sit through another one of your conspiracy theories about how your family was robbed of title? Your family did not have a male to replace your Great-Great Grandfather. Your family's time has come and gone. Deal with it."

"My Great Grandmother had six boys; any of those had the right to reclaim position of second Vezető." Elek shifted his gaze back to Gergõ. "But your family, Gergõ, remedied that, just as the Group of Seven was originally the Group of Thirteen. It is not so whispered behind not so closed doors that this, too, dirtied the hands of the Mátyás family."

"Not all families, Elek, have the ability to lead. Those six families lost sight of our goals and were voted out."

"Not just voted out; they were removed," Elek countered.

"So is the way."

"Your family proposed a secret vote in the middle of the night. You call that the way?"

"Yes, that's correct. And your family was there too, Elek. The Szalai's have as much blood on their hands as every family here."

Gergõ panned the members and looked back at Elek. "So that's it. It is power you want. I was wondering when your envious rat snout was going to free its head and turn on our deal. And there it is." Gergõ walked around the table and stood behind József and Gáspár, leaving Elek on the other side with Henrik and Ákos Simon. "You want to sit in my chair and become Emperor of the world."

"No, Gergõ. We should sit together at the front and run the world as a council. That is our destiny."

"Our destiny," József interjected, "is to prevent that very scenario from happening. We have three letters written on a piece of paper. You say it is legitimate Angelic Script. I see only three letters that hold little significant. And here you are, Elek, already dividing the Group with the promise of ultimate power and world domination."

Ákos stood up quickly, sliding his heavy chair back with his legs. "There is already movement towards a one world government. We have been watching the Masons strategically place their people for centuries, not to mention the Trilateral Commission and the Bilderbergers. Holy szar József, why do you think we started doing the same thing?"

The tension in the room was rapidly thickening; both Gergõ and Elek could feel it as each watched his men verbally defend their own position and then return to assault the opposition. In the meantime, Károly Németh, the oldest and perhaps the most level-headed member, sat at the end of the table. He was the odd man out. The Group of Thirteen was purposely created as an odd number so the council could never stale-mate on any decision; the vote would always lead to a majority.

Károly stood up, walked over to the burned piece of paper, gingerly picked it up, and carefully examined the three letters. As the six pairs of eyes watched his every move, he traced the letters with his finger, feeling the glory of the evidence in front of him and the weight of the final vote. Without saying a word, he carried the paper to a protective glass case that housed the Szentirás Magyar, the original book of prayers written by Attila's own hand with his son Ernak in 461 A.D.

"Károly, what are you doing?" Gergõ barked, his voice full of disdain.

Still silent, Károly unlocked the case and lifted the glass lid, swinging it up on its gold hinges until the arms locked with a securing POP.

The room had become deathly quiet. The silence almost hummed in contrast to the shouting from only a few seconds earlier. Whispering to himself the Attilan prayer for "Wisdom and Guidance," Károly delicately removed the Szentirás Magyar from its glass home. Again, very gingerly, he opened the ancient bible and placed the paper inside of it. Bowing his head, he then prayed to the angel Carviel for strength and guidance so that he might make the right decision. As he closed the sacred book and replaced it back in its case, arguments erupted again between the two sides.

"Gentlemen! Gentlemen!" Károly interrupted, swinging around. "What we have discovered is far too important to make rash decisions. We do need to know if there are any more copies of the script out there. Or if anyone else has this knowledge. I don't believe wiping out an entire village in a moment of panic is a wise choice – yet. I am not ruling it out as an option, but let's not jump right to it."

A grin spread across Elek's face as he watched Gergõ turn deep red with rage. Károly took his seat again at the end of the table.

"We need to send a team back to the village and find out if anyone knows anything," Károly finished.

Gergõ, stiff with anger, forced himself to sit back down in his chair at the head of the table. Elek and Ákos both retook their seats, smug with victory.

"What kind of team?" József asked bitterly. Károly eyed each man and then finally paused his sight on Gergõ.

"Well, we send six Testvériség brothers out as... the Knights of Columbus doing charity, helping them clean up after the fire, spreading the Christian word," Károly said.

"Then?" Henrik asked.

"Then," Elek interjected, "we will have a better understanding of what we are dealing with."

Elek watched Gergõ's eyes calculating his position, his deformed head still red from the stinging defeat.

"Are we in an agreement?" Elek asked around the table purposely avoiding Gergõ. Mutterings once again drifted around the table. "All in favour to send a team say, 'igen (yes).'"

Five of the members favoured the motion. József and Gergõ sustained from any response.

"Good," Elek said, maintaining his dominance in the conversation.

"I want Lukács as one of the team members," Gergõ scowled bitterly, displaying his contempt for the operation and the outright disrespect of his position.

"Ah, Lukács! Your trusted attack dog," Ákos said and then added, "He is more likely to kill the whole village in their sleep, including the other five team members, than to sit on his hands and collect intelligence."

“I trust him explicitly, and if we need a sword…”

“If we need a sword, we vote on it,” Károly injected.

Henrik cleared his throat. “In the meantime, if this small village in Chile was able to carry on this long without our knowing of it, then there may be more.
We need to step up our assignments.”

“The Testvériség is under manned and over tasked already,” Ákos added. “We need to recruit more brothers.”

“And how do we do that?” József questioned. “The Társadalom hand picks the brothers from loyal Magyar families, it is not like we have a recruiting bureau in downtown Budapest.”

“I am just stating a concern,” Ákos fired back. “We’re losing the fight against these abominations. Who knows where and when the next crisis will be. ”

CHAPTER TWENTY-FOUR

Ballina, Ireland
08:05am

Jennifer Leary climbed onboard the 9:05 train in the Ballina Rail Station a full hour ahead of the train's departure time. The 8450 class railcar, which was scheduled to travel to Dublin's Connolly Rail Station, was as basic a rail service in Ireland as one could find. Five seats wide (3 on the right side of the car and 2 on the left) it resembled an average North American subway car. It had no dining car or bar service, just standard seating and a public lavatory. Jennifer scarcely noticed the uncomfortable plastic seat with its compressed and compacted cushion. Her mind was somewhere else and her ass would have to deal with it.

Normally, this time of day was set aside for Jerry Price, the conductor, to do his quick walk-through inspection of the 25 year old car so he could let the maintenance crew know if they needed to do some cleaning, but the earlier trip in from Manulla Junction was empty and the car was still tidy. Since everything was in order, Jerry was easily persuaded by the young lass with long red hair and a pretty smile to claim her seat early. And Jennifer smiled. She was so excited to finally be on her way to Cairo for the Summer Solstice ceremony that she couldn't stop herself from smiling. She needed to get away from the pub that she managed and the constant banging from the construction of the town's new casino-slash-adult entertainment lounge for five sun drenched days in Egypt.

So Jennifer sat alone in the vacant railcar on the two-seat bench by the window. She was filled with nervous excitement and ready to read Midsummer: Magical Celebrations of the Summer Solstice by Anna Franklin. In about 5 1/2 hours she was going to meet her boyfriend, Liam, and four other members from her Wiccan coven at Dublin's

International Airport for her first exotic trip off the Emerald Isle. She pulled her feet out of her shoes and rested them on the opposite seat, grabbed her old, beat-up brown leather travel bag and slid it across onto her lap, fished out her BlackBerry, and texted Liam:

on train. leaving in 60. C U @ airport. Luv U. J.

Jennifer rested her BlackBerry on her bag and stared out the window. She watched a crane high above the village square busily hoisting material against a grey and cloudy backdrop. The idea of this kind of entertainment just didn't sit right with her. One of the most charming aspects of her home town (she thought) was its slow, quiet pace. If someone wanted gambling and strippers they could find it in Dublin or London, but Ballina is a traditional place for fish-n-chips, and a pint of Ballina Ale. A lot less entertaining, but that was the idea, she mused. Even inside the car, the banging and riveting dug deep into her teeth like a dithering dentist performing a root canal. It just may be time to pull out of Ballina all together, perhaps move out to the village of Kells where her coven brothers and sisters live. But in 55 minutes she was going to be whisked away from all the nonsense of building the town's future on bare breasts and slot machines and riding towards an ancient spiritual ground made from the earth herself with the back drop of blue skies and a hot bright sun.

Something outside the car caught Jennifer's eye and snapped her from her day dream. It looked as if the shadows on the crane and construction site were moving and drifting around on their own, detached from their solid masters and defiant against the natural light. The sight gave Jennifer a chill, as though someone had walked across her grave.

A vibrant scent of freshly picked apples suddenly filled the car, and then her BlackBerry started to hum and vibrate.

sorry to hear about the train. fukn delays. would have stayed n waited if u wanted me 2 but will go with jan, rob n group. will wait up for u in hotel in cairo. Luv u back. l

“What?” Jennifer said to herself. “What the hell does that mean? Train delay? This one? I didn’t text that.” Baffled, Jennifer assumed Liam must have received someone else’s text and confused it with hers.

“Excuse me, Jennifer,” a strong masculine voice said from the isle.

“Ahh!” Jennifer yelped, launching her bag off of her lap and her BlackBerry out of her hand; both landing on the floor. Startled and confused at the stranger’s presence inside the car, she must have been deeper into her day dream than she realized to not have heard the heavy metal doors slide open and shut. To her right stood a large bear of a man dressed entirely in black: black over coat, black jeans, and black boots.

“Do I know you?” Jennifer questioned the mysterious man.

“Yes, kind of,” he replied in a strong Middle Eastern accent. “May I sit down?” he asked and motioned towards the empty seat across from her, next to her feet.

“Oh, yes, of course,” she answered and pulled her feet off the bench and quickly slid them into her shoes. Red with embarrassment, she bent down and picked up her weathered travel bag and BlackBerry. On the way back up she looked around the empty car. All these empty seats and he wanted to sit with her?

“I’m sorry, how do you know me?”

The large stranger sat down gracefully onto his chair; the aluminum and plastic frame creaked and groaned under his weight. His piercing blue aquamarine eyes read her, studied her. The scent of apples and apple blossoms grew stronger. As Jennifer watched the dark stranger study her, she didn’t feel intimidated or uncomfortable by him. On the contrary, his gaze comforted her and eased her natural trepidation of being alone with such a large man. She may not have known him, but she didn't sense him to be a complete stranger either.

"Genevieve Cynthia Leary, I am Raphael and I must place upon you a great burden."

What did he just say? Raphael? Unconsciously, Jennifer reached up with her left hand and rubbed the fish charm on her chain around her neck.

"I see you wear me close to your heart, and I hold you close to mine. You have been a loyal and spiritual daughter of the earth and that is why I have come to you."

Jennifer had no idea what to say or how to react to that. Part of her believed someone was putting her on, having a laugh at her expense – which was okay, she knew how to laugh at herself. But another part of her, a very large part, believed the stranger; there was power coming off of him. She had hoped many times that someday she would actually meet an angel or a god. She even prayed to meet the Archangel Raphael. But today? In here? Him?

He wasn't very angelic with biker boots and a pony tail. Where were his wings? His sword? The trumpets or divine glow? Although, his eyes...

"How do you know my name, exactly?" Jennifer questioned, still trying to hold on to some kind of rational thinking.

"Genevieve Cynthia Leary, I am your guardian Raphael. We hold each other close, you and I. You are favoured within my circle. Look within yourself. You know I am not of this world," he replied. His voice became harmonic, penetrating.

"Yes, my Lord Raphael, I believe you," Jennifer said giving up her resistance. "What are you asking of me?"

"I realize you were going on a great and honourable pilgrimage for the Solstice, but I must ask you to place aside your travel for the good of your world, and mine."

Jennifer believed what was happening to her was all part of a dream. The excitement of finally getting a few days off from the hectic pub and going to Egypt to participate in the sacred ceremony charged her imagination, and at any second the train car would lurch on its way to Dublin and shake her awake. Jennifer stared at Raphael, uncomfortably waiting for the train to move. Embarrassed, she looked away and fiddled with her BlackBerry, waiting.

"Genevieve, this is not a dream. You are not asleep," Raphael said, answering her thoughts, his voice light with humour.

"But my coven is waiting for me. Liam is expecting me."

"No, it was I who sent him that message."

Jennifer looked down at her BlackBerry.

"They will pilgrimage to Egypt without you; it has already been written, and your name will live on for all of eternity," Raphael said as he stared into her. "Genevieve Cynthia Leary, your world is about to witness a great destruction from an ancient evil. As a daughter of the Earth and as a priestess under my name, you must help me. You will help me."

Jennifer felt herself give in to the Archangel; after all, who was she to deny this great being.

"Yes, I will help you Lord Raphael."

Pleased, Raphael continued, "Today, a woman, a Canadian woman, will be arriving in Dublin. You must befriend her; she is the key to the coming destruction."

***

Dublin International Airport (Aefort Bhaile Atha Cliath)

Exhausted from sitting and sleeping in three different airplanes, Vivica Papp was thrilled to finally stand on Irish soil, even if it was still inside the airport. Standing motionless, just meters within the airport's departure gateway, Vivica inhaled deeply and exhaled forcefully, allowing her whole self to stretch out into the cavernous terminal that bustles with 20.5 million people each year. Being brushed by the passengers still coming off the BMI flight from her stopover in London, she imagined this was how a boulder felt in the middle of a river during the salmon spawning season. A solid knock from a man who had sat five rows behind her snapped her out of her lull. Taking the hint, she melted into the swimming school of passengers who were making their way down the polished floors of the Dublin airport.

Not interested in the lemon chicken and bland rice offered for lunch on the London flight, Vivica's stomach growled. "Now," she said to no one in particular, "let's get something real to eat."

Up ahead Vivica spied a couple of her female students laughing and flirting with a young Irish man who was selling the standard souvenirs: t-shirts that read "Kiss Me I'm Irish" and "They are Always After Me Pots O' Gold" with a picture of a pot of gold placed over each breast, and plastic 24-ounce pitchers that had "Irish Shot Glass" stenciled on them – Dollar Store items being sold for a lot more than a dollar.

She decided she was too tired and hungry to even bother with them. She was too exhausted from the flights to be the diligent teacher/mother hen who was always trying to guide the young girls away from danger and save their dignity (and whatever else – if there was anything else left to save). Screw it, I'm not their babysitter.

As she walked past she heard one of them say, "His accent is sooo cute," the girls giggled. Like shooting fish in a barrel, thought Vivica.

At 1 p.m. the crowd was intense, both with passengers coming off of flights and others departing. As she repositioned her carry-on over her shoulder, she had to dodge the oncoming flow of people; now she no longer felt like the boulder, but the salmon swimming up against the stream.

"Excuse me! Pardon me! Sorry!" automatically spilled from her lips as the Code of Canadian politeness subconsciously kicked in. Vivica looked down what seemed like a kilometer long terminal for something to eat. The terminal-turned-bazaar had a menagerie of restaurants, coffee shops, souvenir boutiques, and book store outlets: the Caviar House, Starbucks, Burger King, the Bagel Factory... and the Bailey Bar. The Bailey Bar, yes. That's gotta be a good place; after all, it is named after my favourite "get me in the mood" – drink: Bailey's Irish Cream, she thought to herself. The Bailey Bar looked more like a night club than an actual airport pub. A two meter advertisement of a glass of Guinness left no confusion about what to expect on the drink menu. Perfect!

Vivica pardoned and excused her way through and across the near-hostile pedestrian freeway. As she reached the small green and white doorway of the pub, her frustration limit had been reached. Clenching her teeth, she scanned the bar. It definitely looked and felt like a night club. The Bailey Bar carried a strong ultra-modern theme.

The first thing Vivica notice was a large pile of luggage sitting just left of the entrance way. She presumed the patrons placed their belongings there so as not to crowd the floor space. They're more trusting than I am. The second thing she noticed was that it was far larger than it appeared from the terminal foyer, which she now dubbed as the "Great River." The serving bar itself was the entire length of the pub, with an opaque, golden-coloured back-lit wall. It displayed exotic bottles of liquor on clear glass shelves accentuating the European motif. Two twenty-something young men in tight black t-shirts were busy making drinks; the first one poured a clear liquid from a polished, stainless steel shaker into a martini glass garnished with an olive, and the other topped off the head of a pint of Guinness with a three leaf clover. Small black leather settees lined the far wall where a group of young metro couples were merrily chatting away in German. Eight 4-foot tall, long stemmed steel tables, with small round tops and matching stools, filled in the rest of the seating.

Vivica wasn't quite sure if this was her kind of place, but with the cacophony of voices and chaotic activity still going strong in the "Great River," she decided to stay. She walked farther into the pub to the only vacant table and climbed up onto a stool, using the stepping bar to boost herself up. She placed her carry-on onto the opposing vacant stool and thumbed through the menu.

A petit table attendant with short cropped red hair, dressed in a tight, low-cut black t-shirt and black pants placed a 6 oz. glass of Guinness down on the table in front of Vivica, startling her.

"Oh, no sorry, I didn't order this."

"It's complimentary, luv. Plus it looks like you could use a taste," the table attendant replied in her strong, flamboyant Irish accent.

"Me name is Mary, would you be requiring more time with the menu, sweetheart?"

"It has been a very long flight," Vivica confided. "I need something comforting and filling."

"Well, I recommend the Sheppard's Pie. You get a good feast and its piping hot."

"Sounds perfect," Vivica said, stretching a smile across her tired face. She closed the menu and picked up the glass of Guinness. After a large swig she decided it was what she needed.

"Mary, you're right about the Guinness."

The already wide smile on the attendant's face spread even further; she was always delighted when she read her customers right.

"It's like your own wee private spa concentrated down to six ounces. We also have it in a 12 oz. glass, or if you want to soak your feet it has a grand 16 oz. brother," Mary said as a mischievous twinkle flashed in her eye.

Vivica giggled out loud at the thought of 16 ounces of anything, let alone Guinness.

"I think 12 will be grand enough, Mary. Thank you."

"Welcome to Ireland, luv," Mary said and slipped away with a quick wink.

Vivica looked around the modern Euro-styled pub; it was interesting and busy. She spied a woman standing by herself near the bags of luggage at the pub's entrance. The woman was obviously looking for a place to sit. At her side she had a large and heavy looking suitcase with a classic purple Victorian flower pattern. Its handle extended out and there was a worn, brown leather travel bag tightly secured in her grasp. She seemed almost afraid of the noise and activity of the bar.

Vivica wasn't interested in sharing her small table with a stranger (or anyone at the moment) but unfortunately she made the fatal error of making eye contact with the woman. Shit! Vivica feigned a small smile, removed her travel bag, and nodded to the empty stool.

The young woman timorously rolled her purple behemoth over to the small table.

"Aye, thank you very much, luv," Jennifer said smiling as she pulled herself up onto the high top seat. "This pub be brimming over, you could be waiting an hour to catch a seat. My name is Jennifer Leary – and you be?" she asked extending her hand.

"Vivica Papp," Vivica replied shaking Jennifer's hand. "Yes, it is very busy."

To Vivica the woman seemed outwardly pleasant and sociable, but when she touched Jennifer's hand she sensed it trembling. Perhaps she's new to the big city. She's probably over-stimulated by the congestion of the airport, Vivica thought to herself.

"Oh, an American are ya? Flying in for business or pleasure?"

"Canadian, actually," Vivica corrected her. "And I flew in with my class to study the formation of the Giant's Causeway."

"Studying the Clochán an Aifir are ya?" Jennifer smiled and swallowed hard. "I would have thought those stones would have been studied to dust by now." Jennifer gladly accepted her 6 oz. glass of Guinness from Mary and drank it down quickly.

"I will take a grander pint if you don't mind, dearie," Jennifer said nervously.

"Not at all, luv," Mary cheerfully replied with a wink.

Jennifer didn't know what to make of Vivica. Sitting across the small round table from the "key of destruction" (whatever the hell that meant) didn't only make her nervous, it terrified her. Being an alcoholic bar maid that has never gotten into a fight in her life, if this little Canadian woman is powerful enough to get Archangels riled up, what can she possibly do? From the corner of her eye, Jennifer was certain she had once again seen some of the shadows moving illogically, almost on their own.

Vivica tried not to stare at the strange woman across from her, who appeared nervous and unsettled. She was regretting offering Jennifer the stool.

"Are you flying out or flying back?" Vivica asked, trying to be friendly.

"What? Uh..." Jennifer went blank. Was she supposed to be coming from somewhere? She didn't know. She hadn't even thought of an alibi. Fretfully, she rubbed the fish charm on her chain. Then the scent of apple blossoms filled her nostrils, soothing and calming her panicked mind.

Vivica watched Jennifer's tense demeanor relax. "I just flew in from London. I have an aunt who has taken ill there. I wanted to help her. We have very little family in England. But I still have several days of vacation left. Now I need to find some way to entertain myself. I am not really looking forward to resting in my flat quite yet." Where the fuck did that come from? Jennifer asked herself.

That was odd, Vivica thought and took another sip just as Mary delivered her steaming hot Sheppard's Pie and Jennifer's pint of Guinness.

"Have you decided on something, luv?" Mary cheerfully asked Jennifer.

"I'm rain, thank you."

"Are you wearing that perfume? It smells grand. Apple blossoms, isn't it?" Mary asked playfully.

"Um, no it's not me," Jennifer looked around. "It must be from someone strolling by. So will you be staying in the town of Bushmills with your class?" Jennifer quickly asked trying to change the subject. The fact that someone else could smell the apple blossoms made her feel exposed, guilty, like she had been linked as an accomplice from a scented finger print.

Vivica took a sip to clear her mouth full of the Sheppard's Pie. "Yes, I'm staying at the Bushmills Inn while the students stay at the hostel."

"Oh, the Bushmills Inn. Beautiful place. Did you know that it was originally a coach house and stables back in 1608? And the Bushmills distillery was the first legal distillery in the world. You must try their stick toffee pudding; it is so heavenly it will free you from men. Well, unless that man was Liam Neeson..." Embarrassed from her rant, Jennifer took a quick sip of her drink.

Vivica broke the awkward silence. "Actually, I have. I stayed there last year when I came over to study the formations. It is very delicious."

"You have studied the causeway before?"

"Yeah, this is my second time. It makes for a great field trip, but unfortunately the university will only pay for a few days at a time. The geology department has nowhere near the budget some of the other sciences get. How do you know the area?"

"Oh, it's engrained in Irish folklore. I don't believe there is a true Irish lass that hasn't visited the sacred site at least once in school. If you like, I could extend my holiday with you? Give your students a tour with a local flare? Bring them through the legends of Fionn mac Cumhaill or, as the Brits named him, Finn Mac Cool. Did you know...."

Vivica took another bite and then a large gulp of her drink, trying to distance her mind from Jennifer's talking. What did I just walk into? "No, that's okay. I wouldn't want to impose. Plus, we only have a few days and a lot of studying."

"It would be no imposition and I have no other plans," Jennifer countered. That sounded desperate, even to her own ears.

"Mrs. Papp, there you are?" Two of Vivica's students, Becky Bodner and Dianne Weistno, appeared at the side of the table. "I think our bus is leaving soon and we lost half the class and we haven't even collected our luggage yet."

Thank god the cavalry is here. Vivica quickly looked at her watch. "Oh, you're right. We better get going," she said as she waved over to the hostess and fished out her credit card. "Thank you for the offer, Jennifer. I hope your aunt gets better soon." Vivica quickly and gladly signed for her meal and left with the girls.

"Well, I did what I could. I am glad that's over with," Jennifer said to herself. "I can still make my flight with Liam."

Raphael sat down in the now empty seat across from her. "You must follow her to Bushmills. She is the key."

"Couldn't you do it? Strike her down or something. She scares the crap out of me."

"She is only a woman, Genevieve. She is not the ancient evil that is threatening your world. She is the key to saving it. You must follow her and prepare the sacred site. We are on the eve of the solstice and you must do it tonight."

CHAPTER TWENTY-FIVE

"What?" Curtis and Eavery spoke in unison.

Curtis, baffled by the offer, watched the immense weapon float in front of him, the white marbled handle waiting to be received. Jophiel's arm extended out, his powerful hand gripping the blade. In the forefront of Curtis's mind he found it difficult to believe that such an offer was granted to him, that such an honour was being bestowed upon him. In the back of his mind, the practical part of his brain, he examined Jophiel's hand, expecting a significant wound to soon show itself.

"But you just said that only the sword's creator can wield it, and humans can't even lift it. What can I do with it?" Curtis asked still confused.

"Curtis, our blood shares the same source. Your make up, your DNA, is my DNA," Jophiel solemnly replied. The Cherubim's face showed a mixture of both loneliness and separation anxiety, like the face of a lover saying goodbye forever.

"That has never been offered before," Eavery said in a panic from the sidelines.

"That is not true. One has been offered before," Jophiel corrected him.

"Carviel," Eavery reflected. "And look how that turned out."

"How dare you question the actions of an Elohim," Jophiel scolded.

"I'm sorry, Curtis, but that..." Eavery pointed to Jophiel's extended arm, "is not right. The repercussions will ripple through the universe, through all realms, all planes." Eavery turned and focused on Curtis, pleading with him. "Curtis, listen to me, you can't accept that!"

Curtis didn't know what to think. He didn't know how to react. On one hand, he was elated at the honour and sacrifice Jophiel was offering, but on the other he felt the pressure from the wisdom and the concern from Eavery. In the end, the burden to protect his family at any and all costs sealed the deal. Apprehensively, Curtis reached out his hand, grasped the white marbled handle, and retrieved the sword from Jophiel's palm. The large handle made his hands look like a child's. The power and energy of the sword immediately flowed into Curtis's hand, up his arm, and throughout his entire body. It was almost like electricity, but it wasn't the same type of electricity that is used by the radios or S.A.T. phones he commonly programmed back on the base; it was not the man-made industrial electricity that excites and moves electrons. No, this electricity was more of a feeling, a sensation. Like the fresh exhilarating shock your body gets after plunging into a cool lake on the summer's hottest day. It refreshed him. It elevated him as if it was recharging a soul that had only ever been half full.

Curtis held the celestial sword in front of him. He first noticed that the sword weighed nothing. He felt the marble in his palm; his senses told him that it was solid, hard. The shining gold blade with the angelic script was razor sharp and indestructible, and yet somehow it still weighed nothing.

He pulled his eyes away from the weapon and looked around. For the first time he noticed he was in complete blackness. It was less than blackness; he was nowhere. He stood – if in fact standing was what he was doing – in a void. Gone was Eavery and Jophiel, gone was his dining room and home. Gone was the Earth, light, sound. There was only him and the gleaming sword.

Then, far in the distance, a light. How far in the distance he couldn't tell. He had no ability to judge distance or space. It started off as a small pin prick, and then expanded like a train coming towards him down a deep tunnel. It slammed into him: a Roman candle the size of the sun. The rolling wave didn't radiate heat, but instead seeded the cosmos. A tsunami of fire that ignited creation in a symphony of chaos. Before his eyes, Curtis watched the formation of spiraling galaxies and the blooming of gas nebulas as massive stars, planets, and moons populated the empty spaces in between. Directly before him, Curtis watched a molten blob harden to a dark pit. As if flying in an invisible cockpit, an unseen force projected Curtis towards the rock. He stood front row, soaring above as water erupted and churned from hidden depths within its core. Clouds formed above him and torrential rains began to fall all around him. As in past *rememberings*, he was just a spectator, a ghost, and even now he was only a witness. The natural elements never touched him; they only whispered past him.

Violent storms of wind and rain battered the small primitive rock. As the turbulence moved on, or perhaps he moved through it, he watched trees and plants spontaneously sprout from the barren soil like a time-lapsed video on the Discovery Channel. Animals of all kinds, creatures Curtis had never seen before appeared within the foliage.

Curtis watched a gold and marble city take form high above the forest – an Elohim City, the first Elohim City – at least on Earth. It was larger than the city suspended above Halifax; it resembled more of a metropolis. The first golden, mystical, angelic metropolis.

The buildings held the look of ancient Greek architecture, similar temples, arenas, and palaces, but older, more impressive. And he noticed they didn't change and shift like the ones back home. Perhaps that was because Curtis was now high above this city with an unobstructed view and looking down upon it, whereas back home he was always on the ground looking up at it through its cloudy foundation.

Into the distance of the new forest, Curtis could see a defined section all on its own, enclosed within what looked like a gated iron fence. From high above it, he had a spectacular view inside the sanctuary. Springs of fresh water filled the oasis, along with orchards of lush and mature fruit and date trees. He could see two people innocently frolicking and playing. Laughing. Carefree.

It took Curtis a few moments to absorb what exactly he was looking at. Then it suddenly dawned on him that he was looking down into the Garden of Eden, and he just witnessed the very beginning of time, the beginning of Creation.

"I witnessed – the Genesis." The magic of the vision overwhelmed him and flooded his eyes with tears. How could it not? Seeing what no human had ever seen before pulled at him from all directions. He was amazed at what he saw, but at the same time found it impossible to believe he was actually seeing it. He tried to ground himself by brushing the vision off, associating it to some confused brain activity suffered by the electrical shock he received from Jophiel's sword, or, perhaps worse, a full mental breakdown. But he couldn't. What he had seen, what he was witnessing impacted his soul. It blessed him. It elevated him to a higher plane – one closer to that of the angels and perhaps beyond them.

Static condensed in the air, thickening it like the physical manifestation of built up negative energy just before a school yard scrap. He looked around cautiously from inside his invisible chamber as a black menacing cloud covered the planet. Massive bolts of lightning erupted across the sky. Angry booms of thunder echoed off the primitive canyons and mountain tops. Suddenly, a voice pierced the raging weather. A voice filled with hatred, disgust: "I will not bow to them. We are above them."Another bolt of lightning; another thunderous clap.

It was followed by a strong, commanding voice – a voice Curtis knew but had also never heard before, at least not in this life time. It was a voice that was familiar to all living creatures. Just hearing the voice tuned Curtis's soul even finer, like a musician tuning the strings on a violin. It was abruptly replaced by the cackling of three scratchy voices.

"He will never change."

"He is destined to fall."

"Destined to fall."

"Then, you will be beneath them. You have made your choice and the Fates have made mine. You are banished."

A violent crack shook the young Earth and a fiery wound formed at the base of a mountain. Then what looked like a shining star or a burning meteor was launched from a palace within the golden Elohim city. The bright missile impacted squarely into the molten gash.

Curtis watched on as battles began in the streets and on building terraces between the residents of the city. He watched as the physical dimensions of the city shifted and morphed and moved, and how it no longer supported many of the angelic beings. They simply slipped through the floors of the buildings and through the bricked sidewalks and cobbled stone streets as if they consisted of no more than their cloud-like foundations.

Abruptly, Curtis snapped back to his dining room. Still holding the sword, his familiar table and chairs brought him back to the present.

"I…I…" he tried to explain what he had seen but the words failed him horribly.

"I know," Jophiel said, trying to ease Curtis. "I was there when it all happened. I didn't realize by offering you my sword you would have been granted witness."

Curtis turned to Eavery but he was gone.

"He had to… go," Jophiel informed him. "They are odd like that."

Although Curtis was still moved by his experience, the word *they* resonated and bounced around in his brain like a harassing itch just out of reach. Nothing in the house looked any different – except for the missing Eavery.

"How long was I gone?"

"Two minutes."

"Two minutes? It felt like hours."

"Witnessing Creation and the Battle of Angels will have that effect," Jophiel answered. His tone towards Curtis was different now, a little more patient, and more respectful, and *almost* like he was an equal.

"The sword, what do I do with..." Curtis started to ask when it vanished. "Oh, I guess I can make it disappear."

"It will always appear in your hand when you need it, and leave when you do not," Jophiel explained. "Like your thoughts, the sword is yours to control."

CHAPTER TWENTY-SIX

The next afternoon John Christmas pulled up in front of Curtis's house in a red Chevy S10 pick-up truck. The cab's back window was decorated with a mural showing_Darth Vader sitting at a medieval round table with King Arthur, Chewbacca, Captain Kirk, Mr. Spock, Spiderman and several other sci-fi and superhero characters. A large "Vader's Camelot" was boldly displayed across the top of the window. Even though it was a hot day, John wore a long black trench coat and jeans with a t-shirt that read, "And I thought they smelled bad... on the outside." Walking up the driveway, he watched Curtis offer Eavery a beer. Both men were sitting in folding lawn chairs enjoying the June sun.

Billy Idol's "Mony Mony" blasted from a classic rock station out of a beat up radio at the back of the garage. Curtis and Eavery bounced and jived in their seat to the old tune, adding the timeless high school paraphrase to the chorus:"Get laid get fuc..."

"Daddy what are you singing?" Charlie questioned as she walked around the corner. Curtis stopped short the hallowed lexis from his rebellious youth.

"Nothing. Just singing."

As John approached, Eavery leaned over to Curtis. "Have you noticed that guy talks like Spock? I think he's watched too many Star Trek movies."

Curtis gave Eavery a look that indicated he should be quiet.

"Jack Frost, right?" Curtis asked teasingly. Eavery laughed beside him.

"Yeah!" John returned in a feigned annoyance to Jerry Kraft's introduction a few days earlier. "That bastard."

Curtis reached down beside his chair into a soft collapsible cooler. "Beer?" he asked John as he pulled out a bottle.

"Thanks." John twisted the cap off the bottle and took a quick swig.

"So what brings you by?" Curtis asked and then motioned to another folded lawn chair leaning inside the garage. John stepped in, grabbed the top of the chair, and let gravity unfold his seat so he didn't have to put down the bottle.

"A couple of things. One, to see how you were doing and if you needed a hand with anything since your attempted murder yesterday."

"No, I am doing just fine."

"I can see that. Were you not hit by the van?" John questioned.

"Not really; it just missed me. Unlike Brent, where it struck him dead on."

The three men dropped their eyes to the ground as a wave of grief filled their thoughts. A sympathetic and lonely cloud drifting by seemed to pause above the house, adding to the surreal somber tone.

"Are you going to the funeral?" Curtis asked.

"Not a chance," John replied. "You can bet your ass the Testvériség will be staking it out."

Eavery shook his head. "There is something seriously sad about being afraid to go to a friend's funeral."

"That was the other reason I stopped by. I expected you to be barricaded up in your house. I came to offer you a hand if you needed groceries or something – considering Brent's entire family was also..." John didn't finish his sentence.

John eyed Eavery suspiciously and Eavery returned the glare. After a moment, Curtis interrupted the uncomfortable contest.

"We're pretty sure I wasn't the target. I don't believe the KRÁJCÁR know who I am."

"Yet!" John finished. The solitary cloud, picked up by the wind, moved on and once again flooded the afternoon with sunshine.

"Have you talked with your wife?"

"Not yet. She did text my sergeant from London. Her plane was delayed in Montreal," Curtis said.

John asked, "How is your wife taking the news of the 'accident'?"

"Are you kidding? I never mentioned anything to her." Curtis took a sip. "She'd be on the first plane back. Besides, Charlie never even got hurt."

"Not on the outside, but after something like that she might *need* to talk to her mommy, you know. Maybe even to a psychologist."

Curtis gave John a sideways look. "She's safer away from here right now. Was there another reason you dropped in, Dr. Phil?"

John dropped the subject before he started to bring down the mood of the bright summer day; after all, he didn't come out of his way for that.

"Yes. Muin, my spirit guide, told me I should seek you out today. He said that today is the *Beginning*, an *Awakening*."

Eavery sat forward in his chair. "The beginning? Of what?"

John took a shallow sip of his beer. "I don't know. The spirits always talk in half-clues, like Yoda and his riddles."

Concern darkened Eavery's face. "But something is going down today? With Curtis?"

"Yes!"

"Charlie?" Curtis called out, feeling a little nervous and anxious from the news.

"Charlie?" Curtis called again louder. Not seeing or hearing his daughter, Curtis stood up and took a few steps, feeling the residual pain in his feet and ankles.

Eavery also stood up. He extended some hidden psychic feelers around the house and garage. "She's not in your yard."

The three men fanned out around his property, calling her name.

"She is always nearby and she always comes when I call her," the tension peaked in Curtis's voice.

From the road, up the driveway, Sphinx came sprinting past the three men and straight into the garage. All three guys watched the cat and then looked to the road. Charlie was guided across the street and led onto Curtis's property by a stranger's hand.

"Do you know him?" John asked Curtis.

"No, I have never seen him before in my life."

Jake Rogus, holding Charlie's hand, carefully walked across the road and onto the Papp's driveway. His head tilted and shifted from side to side as though a neurological disorder was affecting the motor skills of his neck.

"Charlie, come here, now!" Panic was still high in Curtis's voice. "Thanks buddy for bringing her across the street."

Jake watched as the smiling little girl ran to her dad. Curtis used his fingers like a comb through the front of her bangs. "Why don't you go into the house and play? Maybe grab a juice box?" he said, trying to make his voice sound light and playful so she didn't get the impression that she was in trouble or being scolded.

"Okay, daddy." Charlie looked behind her and waved to the stranger. Jake formed a faux smile and waved back.

Curtis could sense there was something definitely not right with the man. Little did he know, John and Eavery could see both personalities behind the flimsy skin wrapping, a face just millimeters beneath the surface.

"With all the dangers in the world today, what kind of father allows his four year old daughter to play in the street?" Jake chastised, his head canted to the left.

"We should have killed her, strangled her right in the centre of the road," he muttered, disappointed with a lost opportunity.

"Sacred dung of Europa – SHUT UP!" *The **darkness*** said aloud, forcefully straightening Jake's head.

John, Curtis and Eavery watched as the man displayed his internal conflict.

"Is there something I can do for you?" Curtis said as a statement more than as a question and took a step closer to Jake.

Jake ignored Curtis and looked over at Eavery.

"Good day, Brother. It has been a long time."

"Enlil, what are you doing here?"

At the sound of his name, a sudden gust of wind picked up and blew across the four of them standing in the driveway. Jake closed his eyes and raised his arms a few degrees from his sides, spreading his fingers wide and allowing the cool breeze to flow in between them.

Jake's lips formed a satisfying smile.

Curtis looked over at Eavery who was standing rigid and on guard.

"Is he going to be all right? He seemed to have enjoyed that breeze a little too much," Curtis asked. "I didn't know you have a brother."

Enlil opened his eyes euphorically and looked back at Eavery.

"Say my name again, Ea. It has been too long since I've heard it spoken out loud. Say it again and stir the ancient winds. Eavery, is it, now? Ea, Enki, Lugal-Id, Lugal-Abzu, and now Eavery. Am I missing any? Still befriending the puppets, I see," he said and shook his head in dissatisfaction.

Curtis and John looked around as sprigs of corn and wheat began to sprout up in between the blades of grass throughout Curtis's yard.

"Eavery, what the hell is going on? And what is happening to my yard?" Curtis realized that he was missing some vital information.

"He is not who he appears to be," John interrupted. "This tortured man in front of us has another inside of him."

"The Earth worshipper can see me too? What an interesting group you now surround yourself with. What next? Faeries and Leprechauns?" Jake cocked his head. "Let's kill them all!"

"Ahhhh," Jake Rogus bent over and clutched his chest, and then he quickly stood erect like a marionette as Enlil regained control.

"You must forgive my puppet. He has the unrelenting tongue of Venus without any of her other... attributes," Enlil clarified.

"What do you want?" Curtis demanded.

"The good old days," Enlil said, looking back at Curtis.

"Our time has come and gone, Brother. The world has new gods now. New religions," Eavery returned.

"You are wrong, Ea. They are all the same religions, just with new packaging – a kind of extreme makeover, of sorts. The first gods are still out there, and *we're* restless. I still have a job to do. One you prevented me from doing and it is long overdue."

Gods? This guy has lost it, Curtis thought to himself as he eyed the strange man.

"How did you come back?" Eavery questioned, the security of his new friends at the front his mind.

"Well, I hate to admit it," Jake said casually, "but humans have become fascinating. Can you believe they created a device that captures the light from that Egyptian asshole, Ra, as it passes through your water?"

Curtis and John both looked over at Eavery. "Your water?"

Jake cocked his head. "Who the *fuck* are these people?"

"Shut up!" Enlil boomed out loud, pushing Jake deeper within himself and then repositioned his head.

"Why are you here… Brother?" Eavery demanded, looking deep into Jake's eyes to find the eyes of his brother. Eavery purposely avoided saying Enil's name.

Enlil sauntered further up the driveway, closing the gap between them. "They purified your water – made it 'heavy,' I think this puppet called it." Then he gestured up towards the sun. "Humans have discovered that some of Ra's light penetrated deep into the ground, and when filtered through your 'heavy' water, sparks of pure divine energy are created. Not a lot, but enough for one to feed on – you know, build one's strength."

"Surely not enough to bridge the gap?" Eavery returned.

Enlil continued to step and jerk his way closer. "The gap? You're right, Ea." Flowers in the neighbouring gardens sprouted and bloomed as the wheat and corn continued to grow. Enlil continued, "That requires prayer. And in this heathen-rich, technological world, who prays to forgotten gods?"

“Forgotten gods?” Curtis blurted, puzzled by what sounded like nonsense.

Enlil laughed when he saw the expression on Curtis’s face and then understanding lit up his eyes.

“You haven’t told him. This human who smells an awful lot like those half breeds...” Enlil snapped Jake’s fingers, trying to merge the puppet’s brain matter with his own memory. “Analims? Anabims? No, *Anakims*, he has no idea who you are, does he?” Jake’s head shook with disapproval.

“Well...” Enlil motioned forward, waiting for a name.

“Curtis,” Curtis replied flatly.

“Well, *Curtis*, you have unknowingly been in the presence of the great Sumerian divinity, Ea: one of the original deities of you humans. He is the God of Water, Wisdom and Fertility. He is the God of the magnificent City of Eridu on the River Euphrates. He has a soft spot for mankind, is a pain in my divine ass, and he is... my brother.”

Curtis and John turned and stared at Eavery, scrutinizing him, trying to see something divine.

Enlil continued, “Surely, you have noticed that no one else can see him? Not unless he wishes it. Except for this Earth worshipper,” he said pointing to John.

“Which either means you are slipping, brother, or *you*,” he said motioning to John, “are indeed someone I need to keep my eye on.” Then Enlil laughed a hard, exaggerated bellow. “You must have looked like an idiot talking to “Eavery” in public. He doesn’t even have any substance for fuck’s sake; you can pass your hand right through him.” He chuckled some more at the thought. “He’s a ghost.”

“And who are you, demon?” John prodded.

Enlil's face darkened. "DEMON? DEMON? I am no goddamned demon. I am Enlil, King of the Sumerian Gods, the Source of the Ordered Cosmos. I gave mankind plants and cattle and I taught your pitiful ancestors agriculture. You were nothing but wondering nomads before me."

A frosty wind began to shift around the neighbourhood and a small dark cloud formed in the sky.

"He was *also* the God of Famine and Pestilence, the God of Thunderstorms and Floods." Eavery looked around at the changing weather. "You are not planning another flood are you, Brother?"

John closed his eyes, raised his hand and chanted in his native tongue. Quickly, the small cloud thinned and disappeared as the wind died.

"Not so god-like any more though, are you?" Eavery taunted.

A large artery pulsed in the center of Jake's forehead.

"Anyways, I digress. Not long ago, I was hanging out in this hole in the ground, imprisoned between realms, when I felt the familiar tickle of someone's adulation; someone was praying to me. I could tell it wasn't to me *exactly*, but they were using my sculpted effigy, an old figurine swept up from one of my ancient temples, I presume. And my divine intuition tells me that I have you to thank, Curtis," Enlil said looking at him.

Eavery and John questioningly looked over at Curtis. Curtis thought for a moment and then it hit him. "I bought a small stone doll from an old man in Nevatim when I was in Israel. I gave it to a buddy of mine's son, as a kind of neat souvenir."

"Better than that," Enlil said, pulling the conversation back to himself, "you gave it to a troubled, rebellious teenager with connections to the World Wide Web. He held my figurine in his hand and asked me to help him find some stash he lost somewhere in his dwelling. So I helped him find it. Technically, he found it all on his own, but it was promptly after he asked for the help, so I took the credit for it. Now he keeps the figurine with him, and once again I feel the tingles of divine reverence. I will make him my first priest, you know, refresh the lost faith.

My time will come again, and I will fulfill the task that I was given five millennia ago. But if this world is to reap *my* punishment, my flood, I had better hurry, because the First One is coming."

CHAPTER TWENTY-SEVEN

The KACH, short for Kahane Chai (Kahane Lives), is an organization founded by Binyamin Kahane, son of Meir Kahane. The KACH's original goal was to protest the Israeli government's weak stance on a pure Jewish Israel. They rapidly moved to harassing and threatening Palestinian citizens. After the death of Binyamin, the group radicalized and began killing and assassinating Israeli officials who did not support their views.

The KACH was declared a terrorist organization by Israel in 1994.

Hebron, West Bank
Hebron Kosher Meat-Poultry & Deli

The back room of the deli had only one way in and out: a door behind a curtain. Once a store room, it now housed little more than an oval table, a few chairs, and a light bulb hanging on a decorative ringlet chain suspended from the ceiling. Tacked to the walls were large maps of Israel dating from 1990 to 2020. Each map displayed various segments: red indicated Palestinian-owned land, and blue indicated Jewish ownership. As the years progressed, the blue segments increased and the red, in turn, decreased. The final map, dated December 2020, predicted small red reserves locked in a blue Israel.

Joshua Goldstein was wearing camouflaged shorts, a white shirt with "New York Giants" printed down the sleeves, and a stained apron. He sat in a chair that was flanked by two thugs standing behind him. As he leaned forward he rested his forearms on top of the table, anxious and suspicious of the large stranger sitting across from him.

As a member of the KACH, Joshua had been in contact with many pieces of shit from around the world. And on several occasions, some of those pieces of shit were undercover Israeli and UN agents. Once, there was even an undercover Hamas assassin willing to martyr himself (with a tube of C4 explosive inserted into his ass) for Allah and the nation of Palestine.

Joshua was lucky; it happened to be an unusually hot day, and the heat combined with the man's body core temperature caused the C4 to "sweat" and leak out onto the would-be martyr's trousers. The "sweat" spot looked more like a smudge of gooey oil than perspiration, which alerted one of Joshua's men. When the Hamas agent realized his cover was blown, he tried to detonate the C4. A faulty switch was the only thing that saved Joshua and his men, not to mention his deli with a few of its sparse patrons inside. The man was of course shot to death on the spot and then sent back to Palestine with a new remote detonator connected to him. The explosion destroyed the home where the would-be assassin was taken and collapsed the adjacent houses. The Palestinian Authority declared the explosion was an attack from KACH that killed innocent lives, while the Israelis claimed the KACH were defunct and that the explosion was an accidental detonation inside a terrorist cell and no *innocent* lives were lost. Since then, Joshua had learned to trust his instincts.

He sensed a disquieting indifference coming off the stranger as they sat in the backroom with no air conditioning or air flow whatsoever. They were deep in Israel where the air was humid, but the stranger was saturated with the sweet smell of apple blossoms.

Joshua leaned back in his chair, pulled his sleeves high up on his forearm and readjusted the ceramic Glock that pressed under his belt and into his groin. Normally, the cold, solid feel of the undetectable German hand gun steeled his nerves; it helped him feel in control. But this time, he felt it held the persuasive capacity of a child's BB gun, minus the BBs. Essentially, it felt like a clay prop in a cheap movie.

"So, how did you hear of me? And what can you do for me?" Joshua spoke to the man in Hebrew.

The unusual stranger looked like he would have been more at home in a back street roadhouse deep in rural Alberta than in the Jewish quarter of Israel's West Bank. He was dressed completely in black with a black collared shirt, black jeans, leather biker boots, and a large dark overcoat. His long, dark hair was pulled back into a pony tail. The aquamarine blue eyes of the large stranger fell on the tattoo of the KACH symbol on Joshua's right forearm and then shifted to the black swastika tattooed on Joshua's left arm.

"I find it interesting," the stranger replied in the old language, shifting his gaze up to meet Joshua's, "that you openly display a symbol of Jewish supremacy on your right arm, and a symbol that has become synonymous with anti-Semitism and white supremacy on your left. Do you find yourself conflicted perhaps?"

Joshua stared at the stranger so as to project intimidation and power, but as the seconds ticked by and the stranger appeared oblivious, it was Joshua who started to become intimidated. What Joshua wanted to say was, *Enough about me, what the fuck do you want*? Instead, he felt his will power crack, like the fracturing of shifting ice. And, the way a river lets go when the ice breaks, Joshua sounded like a guilty son spilling his guts under the judging stare of his father.

"No. The Nazi philosophy stands for strength, pride... unification."

"Pride?" the large stranger asked, clearly interested on where Joshua was going with this.

"Yes, pride!" Joshua blurted. His two men looked at each other, at the stranger, and then back at Joshua. *Why is he talking about this?* They wondered to themselves.

Joshua wanted to stop talking; the voice in his head even demanded it. But, there he sat, his mouth confessing secret thoughts to this stranger and his two subordinate thugs.

"Pride in purity of race. In purification of country. The Nazi's were cleansing Germany, the same way we need to cleanse Israel. Hitler had an abundance of pride for his race – you can't fault a man for that. It is something that is terribly lacking when I look around *my* neighbourhood."

"It does not bother you," the stranger casually stepped into Joshua's rant, "that there would be another six million Jews in Israel if Hitler hadn't brutally murdered them?"

Joshua stiffened his back. "There wouldn't be an Israel today if Hitler surrendered to political correctness. There would have been no need for Britain and the United Nations to return to us our lost soil. The Jewish sacrifices of World War II, my Great Uncle Eyal, my Great Aunt Sarah, and my mother's Grandmother Adara, all sacrificed. All were shot in their faces and dropped in shallow pits. For what? For being a Jew! They ran a kosher deli in Krakow, Poland. A deli that was in my family for three generations." Tears filled Joshua's eyes. "A deli that should be mine," his voice cracked. "It's a fucking café now that serves tourists.

Believe me, it was a sacrifice set in motion for the House of David to reclaim the Promised Land. Our Land. We are an island of God's people surrounded by fucking Arabs. We were a strong people under Abraham, we were a strong people under Moses, and we will be strong again." He wiped his eyes, cursing them under his breath for betraying his weaker side.

A grin spread across the stranger's face. The spell that held Joshua lifted and the voice in his head that demanded him to shut up regained its control. He blinked and looked back at the two thugs standing behind him. He cleared his throat and pulled his sleeves down, feeling shy and exposed.

"What do you have for me?" he stammered, his voice absent of any authority.

"This." The stranger reached into his coat pocket.

Immediately, the thugs shifted and pointed their automatic weapons. The large stranger, blind to their threatening posture, pulled his hand out. His fingers were wrapped around a small object, concealing it. He extended his arm across the table and laid a small clay figure on its surface.

The figurine was six centimeters in diameter and eight centimeters in length. Most of the characteristics of the figure had been worn smooth from centuries of weather and neglect. The face resembled a gargoyle with large round eyes and a blunt pig nose. Its mouth, frozen into a smile, faintly showed large teeth and fangs and a protruding tongue that ran along its chin. Its head rested directly on its shoulders, and fine etchings within the figurine resembled a right hand holding a sword across its chest and a left hand that held the handle of a digging tool that overlapped the blade of the sword.

"What is that?" the thug on Joshua's right questioned.

Joshua looked over his shoulder. "Shut the hell up." Then he looked back to the stranger. "What the fuck is that?"

"That," the stranger paused, "is your answer."

Joshua stared at the stone doll at the center of his table. It was old, that was without question. It was also ugly-that was obvious, but it definitely didn't look like a weapon. Still, Joshua's instincts told him it was dangerous. He didn't want to touch it.

"A chemical weapon?" he guessed, unwilling to take his eyes from it. He half suspected the doll to spring up onto its feetless, stumped legs and charge towards him.

The stranger continued to watch with amusement the expressions playing across the deli owner's face.

"Is it a biological weapon?" the same thug asked.

"You can't shut your mouth, can you?" Joshua snapped. "Get out of here, both of you. You're pissing me off. Leave me to talk with... what is your name anyways?" he asked. His voice rose with annoyance both because of his men and the apple-scented stranger trying to peddle his discounted wares.

The large stranger, obviously amused by Joshua's frustration, waited until the two men closed the door behind them.

"My name is Chavah," the stranger said, his luminous eyes never leaving Joshua. "And this is no *conventional* weapon."

"It's a clay doll. What the fuck am I going to do with a clay doll? Throw it at them?" Anger bit into Joshua's face as he clenched his jaws. "How is this going to rid me of the rag-heads plaguing my Promised Land?"

The calmness of the abstruse, prodigious stranger unsettled him. With dozens of fire fights and bombing missions under his belt, Joshua was used to being in control of himself.

"Joshua Ephram Goldstein, you are not the first one to lose *The Garden*. Now pick up the talisman. Feel its weight, its strength. Feel how the heat radiates and pulses out of it like the heartbeat from the core of the living earth itself."

Joshua usually launched a verbal assault on anyone who used his full name, – except when it was his mother – but when he heard it come from the stranger's mouth, his hand unwillingly moved towards the figurine. He watched as his arm extended and his fingers approached the doll. With minor obedience, his fingers paused just before contact. He watched his fingers quiver with an anticipation separate from his own desire. Subtly, almost erotically, his middle finger caressed the doll's outer length, like the inexperienced hand of a young teenage boy who was about to touch his first bare breast. His fingers gently circled the dolls eyes and ran along its engraved tongue.

Joshua stared at his hand, confused at what it was doing. He felt something begin to open up deep within him. A feeling of necessity began to grow. He wanted the doll; he needed the doll. Finally, he released the small amount of will power he had left and let his fingers do whatever they wanted to do.

Chavah felt Joshua's submission, and, as he watched Joshua's hand close around the ancient figure, the stranger, with unbelievable speed, grabbed Joshua's wrist and pierced his palm with a small fish bone sharpened to a fine point.

Startled out of his trance, Joshua looked at the stranger and tried to pull his arm back.

"What the hell?"

Chavah continued to stare at Joshua as he easily held Joshua's arm out in front of him.

"No fear, Joshua Ephram Goldstein, it is only a few drops of blood. An ancient ritual of sacrifice."

With the Chavah's grip still solid on Joshua's wrist, Chavah slid his large hand down over Joshua's and began to knead the dripping palm, making sure the blood fell onto the figurine. Feeling like a trapped animal, Joshua tried to pull free, but his arm was frozen in place, separated from his body like a prosthetic limb. Joshua watched as the blood smeared across the stone's surface, and was absorbed into the doll.

Finally releasing his grip on Joshua's arm, Chavah leaned back comfortably in his chair.

"There, that wasn't so bad, was it?"

Joshua immediately withdrew his arm, relieved to be free and have full control again. He exhaled as his panic subsided. A flashing thought of throwing the doll at the large stranger and then shooting him where he sat entered Joshua's mind, but it passed as he realized he didn't want to let go of the stone figurine. Joshua felt the doll warm up in his hand and there was a faint pulsing, almost like a heartbeat, just beneath its stony surface. He eyed the ancient sculpture and stared into its stone face. On a primitive level, he knew the stone eyes of the statuette were staring back. He raised his gaze back to the large stranger sitting across from him. No longer were Joshua's eyes angry and cold; instead, they reflected his insecurities. He now felt humble and small, like a child.

"Now what?" he asked.

Chavah stood up beside the table and, for only the second time since he entered the deli, he freed his gaze from the Israeli rebel and readjusted his black over coat. As the stranger looked away, Joshua felt a heavy weight lift off of him. It was almost like someone removed a wet blanket from his skin. Chavah appeared larger now than he did earlier, almost too large for the tiny back room.

"Now, Joshua Ephram Goldstein, I will call for you when your weapon is ready, but first we need a sacrifice."

"Sacrifice? What kind of sacrifice?" Antediluvian rituals of Hittite priests and priestesses delivering baskets of fresh dates and fish to a stone altar while another sliced the throat of a goat played like a movie in Joshua's mind.

"Human, of course. A powerful human. Only a divine sacrifice can resurrect a divine spirit." Chavah's dismissive tone made Joshua feel used, like a pawn. No, more like a prostitute.

"Who's the sacrifice for?"

Chavah realigned his sight back on Joshua.

"Adam," he said deliberately punctuating his reply. At the mention of the tiny word, the heat that radiated from the figurine began to flow up Joshua's arm and into his body, recharging his hatred for his cause, returning his desire for a cleansed Israel. The doll gave him strength.

Joshua stood up and walked over to the closed door. He placed his hand on the doorknob, but without opening it he asked, "What about help with the Palestinians?" he asked over his shoulder, authority had returned to his voice. When no reply came, Joshua turned back towards the stranger, but he was gone; Joshua stood in the small room alone.

Outside in the back alley, behind the deli, Chavah appeared beneath a small metal awning, hidden from the view of the roof top sentries. As Chavah stepped out of the shade and into the hot Mediterranean sun, with each step, his large, black-leathered persona dissipated away like seeds blown off of a fully bloomed dandelion, and he became a petite, young woman dressed in a long black and gold Islamic abaya gown and hijab.

CHAPTER TWENTY-EIGHT

"The First One?" Eavery asked with a hint of caution in his voice, not certain if he heard Enlil correctly.

"Yes, that's right. The First One," Enlil returned, obviously amused at holding some knowledge that was hidden from Eavery.

"How do you know?" Eavery questioned, apprehension thickening in his tone. "How did *you* come across this information?"

"I still hear the whispers between the realms. You have been on this plane for far too long if your ears have become deaf to them."

"Who is this *First One*?" both Curtis and John asked at the same time.

Enlil savoured the one-up he had on the humans as a small, personal ego boost. It was just another reason among millions why humans were inferior.

"He is An's *only* begotten son."

"Who is An?" John asked, looking at Eavery.

"An is the Sumerian Father God of us all," Eavery answered, all the while keeping his eyes on Enlil.

Curtis did a quick religious reference in his head. An must be the equivalent to the Christian God the Father.

"Jesus?" Curtis asked, not really believing what he was hearing. If this conversation had taken place a few days earlier, Curtis would have dismissed the stranger as a Born Again Jesus lover, but his world had changed a lot since then. "Are you are talking about the second coming of Jesus Christ?"

"No, you stupid human. I'm not talking about your Christ mythology. Whereas Jesus (or his Egyptian alter-ego, Horus) had his divinity entombed in a woman's womb, the First One had his divine essence entombed by the Earth itself. If An, or perhaps you are more familiar with *Yahweh*, *Jupiter* or *Zeus* – not that I care – inserted Himself into the womb of a human woman, His offspring would be like the demi-gods of the Greeks and Romans... Romans, now there was a race that knew how to have a good time. The bathe houses, the orgies, the arenas, the sacrifices..." Enlil's eyes floated up towards the blue sky as he drifted off into nostalgic reverence for the ancient era.

Eavery exhaled loudly with annoyance and frustration toward his brother.

"Enlil? Hello, you were discussing the First One."

A wind stirred around again. Enlil smiled wide at the enchanted breeze and brought himself back to the present.

John clued into Enlil's reference. "You mean the First One was the man made from dust and clay... Adam?"

Eavery nodded his head. "Yes, he does."

Curtis thought back to his experience when he accepted Jophiel's sword. "As in Adam and Eve? From the Book of Genesis?"

"Yes, the first human." Eavery answered with concern still evident on his face.

"Okay, he's coming back from where? Heaven?" Curtis asked, sharing his question between Eavery and the stranger. "Big deal! Why do you look like you just shit your pants, Eavery?"

"Because, Curtis, next to his Creator, Adam is the most powerful being in existence throughout all of the realms."

John too failed to see the significance of Eavery's concern. Although John now worshipped his native religion, he was raised in a Christian home. "Adam is in heaven, paradise. He is probably drinking honey wine and making love to virgins or something. Why would he want to come back here? And why would he pose any threat to the world?"

"Adam never went to heaven," Enlil lectured. "Doesn't every human already know this?" He looked at Eavery for some acknowledgement.

Eavery gave his shoulders a shrug; he thought it was common knowledge too.

"Adam lived until he was 960 years old," Curtis jumped in, his altar boy days fueling the conversation. "He married Eve and had three sons: Cain, Abel and Seth. Seth created the foundation for Judaism."

"Yes and no," Eavery interjected. "After the First One created Eve, they lived together in the Garden for a very long time. Then Eve gave herself to Adam and they had made love for the first time. Obsessing over each other like teenagers, this drew their attention away from An."

"Whoa, whoa! Back this up a minute," Curtis brought his palms up. "You said the First One created Eve. You meant god created Eve?"

Enlil sighed, "No!"

Jake resurfaced and cocked his head. "Let's just kill them right now. They are not grasping anything. We can smash their stupid idiot melons all over the drive way."

John took a step towards Jake and pulled out a twined bundle of sage about the size of a cigar. "How about if I exorcize you out of your own body and leave you as a ghost to wander the streets scaring feral cats?"

"I hate you," Jake hissed before Enlil could reposition his head.

Enlil resumed his sermon. "The First One was powerful enough that he spilled his seed onto the ground and from the dirt formed Eve."

"What the hell did you just say?" John blurted out, unable to contain his surprise. "Did you just say Adam jerked off onto the ground, then played with it and created his wife?"

Eavery shrugged his shoulders. "It sounds crude when you put it like that."

Unapologetic, Enlil countered, "Of course I did. That's how it's done. By the rock ballads of Pan, did you actually believe he used a rib? What the fuck does a chest bone have to do with creation? I can't believe any human actually bought that shit?" Enlil looked around the men questioningly.

"Ea, did it for thousands of years. He is the God of Creation, after all. If you don't believe me oogle it yourself."

"It's Google," Eavery corrected him.

Enlil gave him a sideways look.

"I told you we should kill them," Jake squeezed out.

John and Curtis turned and looked over at Eavery with shocked and disturbed looks on their faces, ignoring Jake's comment.

"It was a different time back then," Eavery said in answer to their expressions.

John diverted his eyes away from Eavery, uncomfortable with the knowledge of Eavery's bedroom secrets, and addressed Enlil. "So after they had sex, they were kicked out of Eden?"

"Yes. Sex was the forbidden knowledge that removed An (or *Yahweh*) as the sole purpose for existence. Roman priests have tried to reclaim celibacy in the hopes of regaining that lost reverence."

Eavery continued, "When that indiscretion, that *first sin*, was created, An pulled out the First One's divinity and sent it to the Nether Realm, limbo, for the rest of eternity as his punishment. His body retained a fragmented soul that eventually died off."

"What about Eve?" Curtis asked. "What happened to her? I don't recall the bible discussing how long she lived."

"That's because she has yet to die. Her curse was to stay immortal. Her divinity was retained."

"Immortality! Living forever! That doesn't sound like much of a curse," Curtis said, still unsure of the new twist on the Old Testament.

Eavery turned fully toward Curtis for the first time since Enlil arrived. "She is the only immortal in her entire family. She watched her husband, her children, and even her great grandchildren die. She has existed on this earth for thousands of years while everyone else has passed on."

"She could always remarry, have more children," Curtis said and quickly regretted it.

"How many times would you watch Vivica and Charlie die before you just stayed away from everyone?"

"That is not entirely true!" Enlil said, watching the conversation.

"What isn't?" the three of them asked.

"She is not the only immortal in her family. Her son Cain has also been cursed to walk the earth for murdering his brother Abel. Personally, I think the annoying dick got what was coming to him."

"You have never had much patience for the humans, brother. Unless, of course, they were offering a sacrifice or prayers, you seemed to always find them annoying. Speaking of which, what is your plan for the one you are possessing?"

"If he can keep his mouth shut long enough so I can reclaim my position and reform the Council of Deities, perhaps I will promote him as a new Angel of Death."

Jake cocked his head slightly with a proud smile on his face. "Angel of Death. I like that – I am coming for you fu... ahhhh!"

"If he can't," Enlil recovered, "I will pull out his own entrails and feed it to him and choose a new puppet. What about you, bear lover?" He said looking at John. "Can I interest you in a new religion?"

John narrowed his gaze. "You have already gone extinct once, are you that eager to return to that hole in the ground? Why don't you go and become lord of some other realm?"

Enlil laughed, nodding his head. "Yes, Lord Enlil. I like it. Perhaps I will drown you last.

But that does bring to mind my new young priest who now holds my idol. It is time I visit him. It is not too late to join me, brother, and once again gain some substance to your *form*. You know, put some meat on those... well, put on some meat."

"Do you mean like what you are doing and taint myself with a poor, corrupt man? No thanks."

"Suit yourself, brother. I'm out of the Nether Realm and I'm not going back."

Eavery softened his posture and took a step closer to Enlil. "Join us instead, brother. If the First One is truly on his way back, this world is finished. Whoever is left won't be worshipping you."

The look on Enlil's face indicated he was considering the proposal. Then his eyes regained their focus and he smiled at the men. "Nice try. First things first: I will dole out my punishment and the First One can have his turn with whatever is left over."

Enlil quickly turned Jake's body, walked off Curtis's driveway and away from the house.

Curtis watching Enlil leave, tried to pass Eavery to stop the possessed man.

Eavery quickly willed his hand solid and grabbed Curtis by the arm.

"What?" Curtis looked back at Eavery, confused. "We can't let him leave," he said defiantly.

John, also concerned, stepped up to the men. "We mustn't let him regain his old self."

Eavery let go of Curtis's arm. "He has possessed a disturbed man and impressed a troubled teenager. He has a long way to go before he re-establishes his old religion. No, he is not our worry yet. We have a much larger problem to concern ourselves with," he said. His tone trailed off as his mind focused elsewhere. "Curtis, I will see you tomorrow."

"You're taking off?" Curtis asked, flabbergasted.

Charlie came back outside with a fruit punch juice box in one hand and snaked her other hand into her father's. Slightly startled, Curtis looked down at the smiling face with a chewed plastic straw between her teeth.

"Yeah," Eavery answered. "I need to recharge my batteries, clear my head. I feel the shit is about to hit the fan."

"Oops!" he said, forgetting about the young ears of Charlie Asia Papp. "Sorry."

Then Eavery turned, and, by the second step, he dissolved into a whisper of air. Curtis found himself in awe as he looked through Eavery until he was completely gone.

John was also shocked at the spectacle. His abilities had brought all kinds of unique and strange experiences into his life since his near death experience and consecration from the Sabáwe Cheboocheech.

"Holy shit! Now that's cool!" John said, astonished at what he would later describe as "evaporated." He looked down at the little girl. "Sorry, Charlie," he apologized.

Charlie didn't seem to have noticed her father's friend's harsh vocabulary. "Goodbye, Enki," Charlie said, smiling and waving her juice box hand. "I like him."

At the sound of his name, the corn and wheat stocks grew several more centimeters; they now stood above Charlie's head.

"Thanks for the crops," Curtis yelled out into the air towards where Eavery disappeared.

"I had better leave too. I will ask the Muin and spirit elders for guidance." John then climbed into his S10 and drove off, taking the long way through the subdivision.

Curtis was left standing in his driveway holding Charlie's hand, uncertain what to do next. The decision-making mechanisms in his brain were still trying to rationalize the last twenty-odd minutes. Then, Curtis's neighbour across the road, Mr. Beverly, a retired marine engineer for the Coast Guard, stepped from the back of his house with a hose with the intent of watering the dying flower garden his wife Linda had planted. Much to his bewilderment, the dying flowers were once again in full bloom, and somehow there were even more of them, a lot more. In fact, as he looked around, he noticed the entire neighbourhood had sprouted similar wild flowers. Mr. Beverly scanned the homes in amazement and spied Curtis and Charlie in their driveway, and then the cereal crop mixture that had overtaken the Papp's once manicured lawn. Mr. Beverly opened his mouth to say something but was so taken aback by the unexpected sight that he just closed his mouth again and began watering the garden, not taking his eyes off the Papps.

Curtis watched the retired old man watching him. Seeing Mr. Beverly's furrowed brow and squinting eyes, Curtis was sure the old man was trying to grasp what he saw. Curtis finally snapped out of his mental leave of absence and blurted out, "Miracle Grow," as a lame explanation. Mr. Beverly nodded with a confused look, and continued watering the flower bed.

***

Later that night, Curtis read Charlie her good night story: *Strawberry Shortcake and the Easter Egg Hunt*. He let her fall asleep resting against his chest, as much for Charlie's comfort of having daddy near while mummy was away, as it was for Curtis's own comfort. He held his little girl, still innocent, still fragile, and thought about what could possibly be the end of all humanity. After Charlie transitioned into her deep sleep and began snoring, he repositioned her head onto her pillow and adjusted the blankets to keep off the cool Atlantic air.

He made his way downstairs, trying to avoid all the squeaky spots on the stairway, and poured himself a large glass of water from the tap. The day's hot sun and the few beers he drank had made his mouth tacky and his body dehydrated. He downed his water and then refilled his glass, turned the light out, and headed into the living room. With a lone table lamp lit and a breeze chasing away the day time heat, the atmosphere was calm and relaxing, which was exactly what he needed while he waited for Vivica's call. She had only been gone for two days, but the whole world seemed to have changed – not that he could burden her with any of it over the phone. She knew nothing about him and Charlie almost being run over by the van, or of Charlie being an ancient Hungarian healer, or of him having Nephilim ancestry and hanging out with a Sumerian god.

But maybe she should. Maybe he should tell her just enough so she would come home and be with them in the world's last few hours. Thinking about it now after the long day, he had doubts it was all real. His reality seemed to be spinning out of control, as if his sanity was rapidly thinning like an old rug whose thread is being pulled. He felt as if soon there would be none of it left. He took another gulp of water and landed heavy on the recliner. He decided he was going to tell her as soon as she called.

As his mind tried to unclutter itself, Curtis began to feel the uncoiling sensation of his senses. The room around him seemed different, almost like he was sitting inside a mirror's reflection of the room. Even though he was comfortable on his large leather recliner, Curtis felt like he was melting within the material. He was slowly and endlessly sliding-oozing into the chair. He watched as the room warped and twisted. His peripheral vision caught glimpses of the walls receding away from him, but when he looked at them the walls would promptly snap back.

Curtis stared down at his legs to try to find some kind of visual anchoring, but they too seemed to stretch away from him, like he was watching the approaching light of a train within a perpetually extending tunnel. It was as if he was falling into himself. Within seconds he had become both Alice and the doorway to wonderland.

Suddenly, Curtis was standing deep in a Yugoslavian forest alongside a large ditch that was filled with dead bodies of all ages. On the opposite side of the ditch he watched a dozen camouflaged, grey uniformed men shoot point blank at what appeared to be a family from a nearby village. Shock, disbelief and despair smacked him as their bodies fell dead into the horrific mass grave. Curtis screamed. He looked around in his panicked state for someone to do something. Instead, two more military group transport trucks that were filled with more villagers pulled up alongside of the uniformed men.

A line of people outside the trucks stood waiting their turn. The solemn look on their faces said they were already dead. A boy of fifteen broke from the line and ran for the cover of the nearby trees. An armed sentry standing on top of the truck's cab quickly took aim and gunned the boy down. The families screamed and cried as the boy's body dropped. At the front of the line, a father in his forties held his five year old son in his arms. Curtis could hear the father reassuring the boy that everything was okay as his son sobbed heavily into the nape of his neck. His wife walked behind him clutching their twelve year old daughter. Another young couple, maybe eighteen years old, was being pushed up behind them. The young woman was dressed in a long maternity gown and looked to be several months pregnant. A soldier, bored with simply standing around, swung the butt end of his AK-47 machine gun into the back of the head of the young man. As the young man dropped to his knees, the soldiers laughed and yelled at him to keep moving, one soldier off to the side planted a solid kick into the man's ribs while he was trying to get up off the ground. The pregnant teenage girl screamed and desperately tried to lift her lover back up to his feet as the soldiers mocked and laughed at them. Two soldiers watching looked the young woman up and down. One leaned in and whispered something to the other and they laughed out loud. Curtis somehow knew they were deciding if she was good enough to keep around for a while (maybe a couple of days) before she too would fall down into the ditch beside her boyfriend – or beside someone else from another village.

"What is going on?" Curtis screamed out. The horror and brutality was inhuman. The carnival-like exposé the soldiers displayed towards the massacre of these people, these families, not only disturbed him, but it also felt like it was scarring him. Curtis knew he was trapped within the *remembering*, but whose? And why? Only minutes ago he was sitting at home in his chair beginning to feel lonely and sorry for himself, and now he was watching this massacre, this... genocide.

Crack-crack-crack.

Twelve shots total sliced through the wilderness. Curtis, unable to pull his eyes away, watched as several whole families collapsed into the pit. All were shot in the front of the head (to see it coming).

The next group was pushed away from the trucks towards the edge of the ditch. Again, the rifles took aim. The young boy clung to his father's neck. Quiet now, he simply stared down into the pit at the bloodied bodies and dead expressions. The father held his daughter's hand and she gripped tightly with her other hand to her mother. Forever united.

Crack-crack-crack.

This time thirteen bodies fell into the trench. The teenage girl screamed in horror as she witnessed her family, her soon to be husband, and her neighbours being murdered, and then she screamed again when two soldiers dragged her off behind the truck.

Overwhelmed by sorrow and revulsion, Curtis dropped to his knees at the side of the pit and vomited. Curtis's physical body, still sitting in his recliner, also reacted to the *remembering*; he convulsed and vomit sprayed all around him.

Still trapped in his vision, he waited for the *remembering* to finish. Instead, in an instant, Curtis flashed from the Yugoslavian forest to the desert roadside. With the intensity of the previous vision still gripping his mind, it took him a few moments to recognize he was back in Afghanistan.

He was at a roadside check point, cement barricades with a cheap portable booth, 23 kilometers outside Kandahar. He was standing beside his buddy, Ryan Switching (a.k.a. Switch), a corporal with the 2 RCR (2nd Battalion Royal Canadian Regiment from CFB Gagetown, New Brunswick). Ryan was doing another standard search of vehicle number seven (every seventh vehicle was getting checked that day; the day before it was every four vehicles, just to keep the Taliban guessing).

Curtis's heart shifted from the revulsion of the genocide to grief as he looked at a friend who was killed in 2004 during Canada's contribution to the war against terrorism. The two of them quickly became good friends, and even made plans to get their families together on holidays when this shit was over.

Curtis stared at Switch; he looked just like he did back then. During a check point search, a man in a sand-blasted yellow Toyota Tercel blew himself up along with Ryan and two other Afghan guards. Curtis watched the whole thing happen. He had been called out from Kandahar City to fix the communication link at the check point. As Curtis bent down to get a screw driver from his tool box, he saw out of the corner of his eye the yellow Tercel pull up to Ryan and stop at the check point's control arm. Curtis hadn't paid much attention to the driver at the time; a combination of the heat, the sand, and the fine talc-like particles that got into all of his tools and equipment was all Curtis could think about (and getting his ass back to base). In the tens or maybe hundreds of replays that have since plagued his dreams, Curtis remembered (or thought he could remember) the look on the bomber's face; he looked nervous, scared, and perhaps he even changed his mind. He didn't have the cold look of a man determined to rid the world of more infidels and guarantee his place with Allah. But with the Taliban, it didn't really matter. If the bomber changed his or her mind, they detonated the bombs remotely anyway (a little trick they like to keep to themselves).

Good old Switch was a true Albertan. He loved his Molson Canadian, his skiing, the Army, and he loved to hate the band Nickelback. Curtis never made it to Switch's funeral. Even though the blast was mostly deflected by the cement barriers, the shock wave threw him nine meters down the road. He dislocated his left shoulder, cracked three ribs, and ruptured his left ear drum. Curtis had lain in a hospital bed in Landstuhl, Germany, and watched the repatriation ceremony on T.V. Switch's casket, covered in a Canadian flag, was carried down the ramp of a C-117 Globemaster back in Trenton, Ontario. As the camera panned the ceremony, it stopped and zoomed in on Ryan's widow, Karen, and his two young children, Serena and Ryan Jr. Just thinking about Ryan's children growing up without their dad still brought tears to Curtis's eyes, and that usually led to a day of over-affection toward Charlie.

That day would live forever with Curtis. He had never felt more alone and terrified in his life. As Curtis bent over to reach for a Philips screwdriver, he turned his head and watched as Ryan cautiously approached the driver's side window. Ryan was smiling, as he always did to help keep the civilians calm and to prevent himself from going insane. Curtis actually thought, "Here's another boring and routine job," and bent down another ten centimeters – ten life-saving centimeters to grab a screw driver.

KABOOM!

Flashes of sand, sky, and blackness are about all Curtis can remember of the time before he was medevaced out of the zone – not that he tried to remember or even wanted to.

Now, Curtis stood there again seeing the smiling face of his dead buddy. Curtis smiled too, in spite of the sorrow flooding his heart: sorrow for a missed friend, and sorrow for the family who lost a husband, a father, and a son. Curtis also felt self-pity for almost being killed too, and for the pain that Vivica and Charlie almost had to endure. Tears streamed down Curtis's face as he stood there once more. His body, back in his home, sitting down on the recliner, sobbed and shook uncontrollably. The hand that held the glass of water trembled and water spilled onto his lap, the chair and the floor.

Deep into the *remembering*, Curtis stood there staring and missing his friend. He knew what he was looking at was just a replay, an echo of his friend from years ago. It may not be real, but the *remembering* was making it feel like it was happening all over again.

Then something moved behind Switch's back. Curtis focused off his friend's face and looked beyond him. His heart stopped. Dread overpowered the feelings of sorrow and loss. Panic replaced Curtis's tears when he realized he was staring at his own face inside the check point guard house. Curtis numbly turned to his right and watched as a yellow Toyota Tercel pulled up beside them. He watched as a smile stretched across Ryan's face. He watched as the sweaty driver nervously tapped his fingers on the steering wheel as if drumming to a song playing in his head. In slow motion, Curtis watched Switch bend over to talk with the driver and he saw his earlier self bend down to get the screwdriver.

KABOOM!

As the bright white flash faded, Curtis once again sat in his chair back in his home. His heart was beating out of control and he felt as if he was on the verge of cardiac arrest. His hair and back were soaked with sweat, his face was wet with tears, and his shirt, shorts and legs were covered in vomit. The glass of water was no longer in his hand, but lay broken on the floor beside the chair. He sobbed uncontrollably, trying desperately to compose himself. A quick look at the clock on the wall told him that the *rememberings* lasted for almost 70 minutes.

"What the fuck just happened?" he said aloud, a combination of drool and vomit spat out of his mouth as he spoke. Looking around the room to help ground him in the present, he noticed for the first time how wet his shorts really were. Curtis couldn't be sure if it was just water from his glass, or if he pissed himself – probably a little of both.

With shaking hands, he wiped his chin, grabbed the arm rests of the recliner, and pushed himself up onto weak legs.

"The Jinn seem to have that effect on humans," said a calm, sultry, and almost angelic voice.

Startled, and in a hyper state, Curtis snapped his head towards the kitchen where the voice came from. The kitchen was pitch black; no ambient light from the neighbour's back deck or stray rays from the street light out front seemed to penetrate the windows or the side door. Even the soft glow of the living room lamp stopped at the door frame, unable or unwilling to cross the threshold. The first thing Curtis saw were two red eyes beaming through the velvet blackness. Solid. Still. Terrifying.

CHAPTER TWENTY-NINE

Curtis's heart raced again, thumping heavily in his chest. *Will I need Jophiel's sword?* Curtis wanted to move, but he couldn't. He wanted to yell at the stranger, threaten him – or it – to get the hell out of his house, but Curtis couldn't do that either. Curtis wasn't sure if he was spellbound or just terrified; he only knew he could not move. The two eyes shifted in the darkness. They waved slightly from the left to the right as they moved closer until a form pierced the light of the room. The blackness of the kitchen held onto the contours of the stranger's face and body like a jealous lover. Curtis could tell the blackness wasn't merely a harmless shadow, but a living entity unto itself. It bent and moved, and almost stretched to stay in contact with the stranger. The blackness looked as if it caressed his skin as he pulled through; it cried and whined in a multitude of high tinny voices, but eventually receded back into itself_within the door frame. The stranger's entrance into the living room was terrifying in itself.

As the stranger approached Curtis, every emotion Curtis had ever experienced surfaced, but then was quickly replaced by another emotion again and again. The constant emotional turnover paralyzed him; it prevented his cognitive faculties from grasping and analyzing the situation. It kept Curtis helpless, trapped within the very essence that made him human.

The stranger was six feet six inches tall, muscular, and thin like an athlete. His skin was the colour of bone bleached by the sun, and he had a familiar marbling just under the skin, just like the angels, but it was gold instead of Jophiel's silver. His hair was long, straight, and pure white. His eyes and the nails on his fingers and toes were a brilliant red, and he was completely naked except for a white leather belt that was strapped up across his chest and around his waist, which secured a golden scabbard. A disproportionately long member hung unabashedly between his legs. He had no pubic hair (or any other hair but what lay on his head) anywhere on his body. The sword handle looked like it was made from bone or ivory, and a quick glimpse revealed a shining and glittering blade. He walked with the grace and confidence of someone who has never feared anything.

"Who are you?" Curtis managed, forcing the words out.

The graceful and beautiful Being continued to approach him.

"Hello, Curtis. I have been hearing a lot about you," the stranger said, toyingly. "How rude of me," he continued, his red eyes penetrating Curtis. "I am Ha-Sata, the Shining One. But you may call me Lucifer."

Curtis's world stopped when he heard the name. Until this very moment, he wasn't sure if he even believed in a Satan, in *any* Satan. He had convinced himself long ago that this particular supernatural being was folklore, a mythological fairy tale. Throughout his whole life he had heard stories of the evil Being: the greatest angel who defied God – the first angel to defy Him. He was the one that was cast down into Hell to reap the souls of sinners. Until now, it seemed all too ridiculous. Satan was supposed to be a metaphor for the negative side of the humanity, the ever-existent dark side of man. Curtis believed Satan was the boogeyman that the Church created and used to threaten its flock into submission. Until this moment, the left side of Curtis's brain – the side that controlled rational thought and reasoning, science and technology – mocked the old religions, the old mythologies. Until this moment.

"But then again, we have already met. You had better breathe, boy," Lucifer said waving his hand and ceasing the emotional firestorm that had paralyzed him. "You are better to me alive."

But the fear still gripped Curtis. A super-imposing fear that transported Curtis back to when he was five years old and frozen beneath his covers after having a night terror. The immobilizing fear experienced by the young Curtis once again pumped through his veins.

He had dreamed that the devil in all his horned and bat-winged glory held Curtis upside down by his ankle over a cavernous lake of liquid fire where tortured bodies twisted and screamed in pain. The smell of their burning flesh and hair followed Curtis for days afterwards. The stench clung to him at school, at the supper table, and even at Church on Sunday. When Curtis discussed his dream with his parish priest, Father Sullivan, the priest told him his dream was caused from the guilt of a sin he committed (probably the deeds of a bad boy against his parents), and God was telling him to repent. As soon as Curtis was of age, he became an altar boy, hoping the good deed would cancel out any previous adolescent indiscretions.

A nightmare seen through the eyes of a child was like as an *actual* encounter with Satan. As Curtis matured, he looked back at that encounter as a horrible dream seeded in his impressionable psyche by the very Church he had grown to hate. And until this moment, that experience had remained a horrible dream. The putrid smell of charred flesh once again returned to his nostrils.

"That wasn't a dream," Curtis realized in astonishment.

"No, I don't have to appear only in dreams like some of the lower class," Lucifer said, referring to lesser angels. His bare feet caressed the floor as he stepped closer to Curtis. From under the furniture shadows reached out longing to touch him.

Curtis felt an unbelievable force radiating out from the fallen Seraphim even hundreds of times greater than what he felt from Jophiel. He could feel his energy engulf the entire house. He sensed it piercing the walls, the individual shingles on the roof, and even himself. The ancient, indescribable energy formed a bubble around the house, insulating them inside, isolating them from his neighbours and from the rest of the world. Rapidly, the room dissolved, not pixelating away like the transitioning phase of a *remembering*, but melting away like plastic in a brilliant display of ooze and fire.

Again, Curtis was before the cavernous lake of fire and tormented souls, but this time he was standing at the edge beside the devil as a 34 year old man. The heat pummeled his bare skin on his face, arms and legs.

"Do you remember this place, Curtis? Of course you do. No one ever forgets the sight of Hades."

Curtis tried to pull and tug his eyes away from the fire and challenged himself to look at his "tour guide." Satan still looked as he did back in his home – naked with no horns or wings like in Curtis's childhood experience – but now his eyes and nails were a deep black. Bombarded with fear, shame, embarrassment, and guilt, Curtis relived memories of the lying, cheating, and pain he inflicted on others throughout his life. These were nothing really serious at the time, but now collected all in the same moment they became strong and heavy.

He tried to muster some courage to confront his escort, some defiant anger he could hold onto, but it was pulled from him. Every breath, every exhale seemed to leave him with less... soul.

"The weight of guilt and judgment is heavy, isn't it?" Lucifer stated more than questioned. "I am going to tell you something very few others seem to realize. Guilt and all its weight, Curtis, is not from Him," he said pointing his finger and blackened nail towards the cavern's ceiling, "or from me." Lucifer's black eyes penetrated Curtis. "They're yours. You willingly judge yourselves at an unachievable standard. Even the *precious* saints tormented themselves with it."

Curtis looked back down at the twisting, deformed figures, expecting at any moment to be tossed in among them.

"Don't worry, Curtis, I'm not here to hurt you."

Fear for Charlie flashed through Curtis's heart.

"Or Charlie."

"Then why are we here?" the words were tight in his throat.

"Because an old acquaintance of mine is trying to come back to your realm. And if he succeeds, your world – the entire world – will change as you know it."

"Yes, I have already heard," Curtis said, still watching the lake of fire. In less than a second, Curtis was standing back in his living room, away from the melting cavern walls. Feeling more at ease now that he was back in his own home, Curtis tried to put the day's pieces together.

"Enlil wants to punish the world," he finished.

"I am not referring to that old has-been. I am talking about the First One."

"How can whatever Adam do be worse than Enlil flooding the globe?"

"A flood," Lucifer chuckled. "A flood will kill millions of people, perhaps a billion. And when they die they will be judged and a majority of them will come to me." The intensity of his red eyes flared at the thought of fresh souls. "But if the First One comes back, he and Eve will recreate Eden."

Slowly, heartbeat by heartbeat, Curtis gained his composure. The overwhelming radiating power that emitted from Satan was either ebbing or Curtis was unknowingly learning how to manage its effects.

"Bringing Eden back to the world doesn't sound so bad," Curtis said, more relaxed now. "Actually, it sounds like a wonderful idea. Is that why you don't like it?"

Lucifer traversed in front of Curtis like an attorney laying his case. "The re-creation of Eden will absolve original sin."

"So?" Curtis questioned. It seemed to him that each point Satan made drew Curtis more to Adam's side.

"By the Creator's own law, Eden makes humans immortal. And if they never die, there is no need for a heaven or a hell." Lucifer let the last word hang in the air.

"I'm liking Adam more and more," Curtis candidly replied.

"In Eden," Lucifer continued, frustration creeping into his voice, "humans are created by Adam's own seed. That means no more births, no more children. Charlie will never grow old – only stay as she is forever. She will never have children. You and Vivica will never have grandchildren. It is..." he paused for emphasis, "unnatural."

That is unnatural, Curtis thought, *but words from Satan cannot be trusted; they are always double edged.*

"So no more souls feeding Hell... Hell dries up and the universe is better for it," Curtis said, feeling stronger with Adam as a weapon.

"Hell was created to balance the universe. How can you judge your actions to be honourable if you cannot weigh it against dishonour? Without judgment there is no responsibility. What would your new world be like if not one soul was held accountable for his or her deeds? In the new Eden, human nature will not change; your tyrants will remain tyrants – forever. And the souls," Lucifer turned his hands over with his palms up to pantomime a scale, "who are neither good nor evil will be without a line in which to keep them 'balanced.'"

The complexity of human nature and its position in the world was greater than Curtis could have imagined. "So then, why don't you stop him if it's such a bad idea?" Curtis asked, motioning towards Lucifer's sword.

"After I deceived Eve and the First One, which led to their legendary expulsion from Eden, Yahweh forbade me from ever coming in contact with them again."

"You could send a demon after him."

"I do not have a Lieutenant in my ranks that I trust enough for such a task. Not that it would matter. I could send an army of demons and he would walk right through them."

"How is that possible? How can he be that powerful?" Curtis asked, not sure if he believed Satan's tale.

"He was the First One created in His own image. Even I do not hold that honour. Outside of Yahweh himself, I am the only one who is capable of defeating Adam."

"So why have you come to me? What could I possibly do?" Curtis asked. Insecurity and suspicion wormed its way into his thoughts.

"When I held you by your ankle, dangling you over the edge, I could taste Jophiel in you. I knew some day we would be working together. That is why I spared you."

The fiery image caused Curtis to begin shaking. "Why should I help you?" he said, faltering.

"You mean besides the whole 'balance to the universe' scenario?" Lucifer returned.

Curtis just stood and swallowed hard. Lucifer casually looked around the room and spied a recent family photo. Curtis followed his red gaze.

"She is beautiful. Has she called you yet from Ireland?" Lucifer returned his gaze back to Curtis. The thought of Satan keeping an eye on Vivica sank heavy like a stone in his stomach.

"Yesterday, a witch priestess, deceived by Eve, befriended your Vivica. And today Vivica is being held by Eve and her people on the open face of the ancient altar commonly known as the Giant's Causeway."

"The Giant's Causeway?" The words rattled in Curtis' head. "She's there studying the rock formations."

Lucifer elegantly snaked over to the portrait of Vivica and gingerly picked up the wooden frame. His eyes caressed over the details of her face: the oval contours of her brown eyes, the delicate bump of a nose, the full and smiling lips. A slight erection formed as his penis began to swell. He knew, of course, that he was displaying himself in front of Curtis. He was purposely pushing him. He wanted Curtis to become jealous. Jealousy will breed anger and anger will strengthen Curtis' natural instincts to protect his family. Yes, he could feel his little ruse working on Curtis; he could feel the anger begin to pulse inside of Curtis.

Pretending to be unaware of Curtis, he continued, "Ancient man watched giants hurdle down from the sky onto those formations. To them, these giants leaped across the causeway from Scotland. But those stone formations are only one of a few locations on Earth that act as a doorway to other realms."

Lucifer carelessly dropped the picture frame back down onto the end table the way a child would reject a broken toy. Curtis watched as he discarded the picture and a stronger surge of anger bubbled in him. The sound of the glass pane rattling dangerously inside the wooden frame rattled deep down his own spine. He stared at the picture of Vivica as she smiled. Curtis wanted to step across and pound some respect into the pasty white asshole.

Lucifer felt the toss strike the mark he was looking for. Curtis was angry now – good. Acting as if he didn't give a second thought to the picture, Lucifer casually turned back to Curtis.

"And what the ancient humans perceived to be a bridge was actually a ladder. And the legendary giants were realm Beings, mostly angels, but they soon became Druidic Gods."

"A Jacob's Ladder?" Curtis asked.

"Yes, the ladder with which the Jewish patriarch Jacob watched angels descend from Heaven in his dream."

"If the old druid gods could descend the ladder, why does Eve need Vivica?"

"The First One's divinity has been banished from this realm. It will require a human sacrifice to bind him here. And his divine soul will require a human host."

Like being woken with a splash of cold water, Curtis figured it out. "Are you saying Eve plans to sacrifice Vivica and Adam is planning to possess me?"

Lucifer watched the reality of the situation spark a troubled look across Curtis's face. He allowed Curtis to stir in his thoughts for a second longer.

"Not exactly."

"What do you mean, 'not exactly'?"

"A mere human isn't a great enough sacrifice for him. No, Eve needs a divine-*ish* sacrifice."

Curtis was still a little confused. And then it struck him.

Lucifer continued, "They are using Vivica to get you to that circle, Curtis." He casually walked around Curtis again. "They have already selected their human host," Lucifer said, sounding almost enamoured with Eve's plan.

Curtis followed him. "So how am I supposed to kill Adam when nobody in heaven or hell can?"

"With my sword," he replied, energized at the thought of battle.

"What?" Curtis said, stunned at Lucifer's answer.

"Yes. You must strike him and his host at the same time, and only my sword will kill him once and for all."

Curtis stood across from Satan truly taken aback by his offer.

"Do we have an accord, Curtis?" Lucifer asked in a very business-like tone. "Will you accept my offer to help you save your world and your wife?" Satan extended his right hand in a gentleman's fashion.

Curtis couldn't think clearly. Too much had already happened within the last thirty-six hours – first with Jophiel, and then Enlil, and then the *rememberings*, and now Satan. This must be a bizarre dream. He stared down at Satan's extended hand, at his pale skin and perfectly manicured black nails. He knew in his bones that he should not shake hands with the devil – Satan always held a trick up his sleeve – but Curtis believed him. He believed Lucifer needed him and that he also needed Lucifer. Satan may speak in half-truths, and even though Curtis suspected there was probably more he wasn't being told, he was sure the information Satan was telling was the truth. He continued to examined Satan's extended hand, and glanced over at Vivica's picture, which, somehow, miraculously, was properly standing again on the table. *She hasn't called me yet,* he thought to himself. *Right now they have her.*

"My sword, Curtis, is the most powerful weapon in existence. It can even help protect your family – your daughter – from the KRÁJCÁR."

Lucifer's words struck Curtis where he was most vulnerable. "You won't need to run anymore, Curtis. That's what you want, isn't it... to stand and fight? Take it!" he said, and flexed his open hand.

Curtis's mind raced. Memories of holding Vivica's hand flashed to the surface. As though a video reel was playing before his eyes, he watched his wedding: their first kiss as husband and wife, their first dance. He watched the very first time they made love together... and also the last time. And, out in the distance beyond the image of his wife, he heard the soft snores of Charlie peacefully sleeping upstairs in her room. Now the memories of her birth filled him. He watched himself holding her tiny, flannel-wrapped body inside the delivery room when she was only seconds old. The overwhelming joy of that day pulsated through him as he stood in front of Satan.

Lucifer's face held the expression of an honest and concerned used car salesman.

Then Curtis saw a slow replay of the white van striking Brent just inches away from Charlie. Curtis heard the vulgar snapping of Brent's bones as he connected with the van's front grill and bumper, and the expression on Brent's face at the moment of collision. Curtis saw Brent's limp, rag-doll form as it flew helplessly through the air and he heard the wet meat sound as Brent collided with the metal lamp post. Curtis then focused on the cold-blooded murder of Brent's wife and son. He looked again at Satan's extended hand. He could still hear Charlie's soft snores. And that sealed the deal – Curtis must protect her, even if it meant selling his soul.

Curtis extended his right hand and slid it into the palm of Lucifer's. Satan's smile widened. "Then we have a pact."

A question immediately popped into Curtis's mind. "How will I be able to use your sword? Humans can't just pick it up and wield it around. I would have to be a descendent of yours and we know that's not true."

Lucifer continued to smile and stared directly into Curtis's confused eyes. He tightened his fingers around Curtis's hand like a boa constrictor. Each finger grew longer and extended in length. Curtis looked down at his hand; there was something odd about Lucifer's arm. Something bulged and moved under his skin, and then the head of a red snake broke free.

A red serpent with black diamonds along its back fought the skin of Lucifer's forearm and slithered out of the ruptured lesion. Curtis watched as the small snake, the size of an average garter snake, coiled itself around Satan's wrist and then made its way across his fingers and onto Curtis's hand.

"Then you will have to possess some of my DNA also," Lucifer confessed.

Curtis couldn't believe what he was seeing, or what he'd just heard. The black, diamonded serpent slithered further onto Curtis's side of the handshake. He tried to pull away – sort of – but his arm was frozen in place; he was frozen in place. The beat of his heart slowed down at the sight of the encroaching snake. He couldn't help but hold his breath and watch in terror as the most perverted of creatures inched its way toward him. The snake eyed him, too. As it slithered forward, its forked tongue darted out and featherly touched his skin. The snake felt cold as it made contact with Curtis as it slid across the bridge of his thumb and forefinger. He could feel the grip of its scales as it pulled itself forward onto his wrist. Then it stopped; its tongue continued to probe the air, smelling, tasting. It stared at Curtis, into him, reading him.

Curtis was sure the snake was going to lunge at his face, and there was nothing he could do about it. He would stand there, immobilized by Satan's grip for eternity, taking whatever assault the black and red serpent decided. Instead, it looked down and examined Curtis's forearm. He watched the snake as it slid down another inch and began to push its face into the skin of his arm. At first, Curtis thought the snake was scratching itself, but then it broke the skin. It continued to work the spot and make the wound larger.

What the fuck is it doing? he thought as he stared up into Satan's face. Lucifer's expression showed that he was very pleased with himself, and the snake.

The pain in Curtis' arm became excruciating. He looked down just in time to watch the snake force its head under his skin and into his arm. The body of the serpent still gripped his wrist and fingers as it continued to force itself in deeper. Curtis couldn't believe his eyes as he watched his own skin stretch and expand from the body of the snake. Inside Curtis's head he was screaming in agony. He felt the snake's nose push aside tendons and muscle as it worked its way in between the radius and ulna bones of the forearm.

Tears, the only way to physically express the torture Curtis was going through, streaked his face. If he was strapped to a bed and tortured to the same level of pain, he was sure he would have passed out by now, but Satan forced him to endure it – no getting out that easily. Curtis felt the snake continue further into his arm and then watched as the skin bulged on the underside of his arm. It was working its way back towards his wrist.

Lucifer unwrapped his fingers and let go of Curtis's hand as the last of the serpent slid across his own. Satan stood there, his black eyes gleaming. Curtis still couldn't move. He continued to feel the burning pain of the cold snake slithering through the meat of his arm, its scales gripping and pulling itself along. He watched the bulging of his skin as the serpent pushed up the center of his wrist. Finally, in the middle of Curtis's palm, the serpent broke the skin again and pushed its nose out, wiggling and tugging to free its head.

Blood ran down the palm of Curtis' hand and onto the floor. As the snake's head breached the skin, it opened its mouth wide. With its head in Curtis' palm, and most of its body still inside his arm, the remainder of the snake (its tail) rested on the first metacarpal (or knuckle) of his index finger. Curtis stared in disbelief at his arm. The cold, yet burning pain now consumed his entire body. Before Curtis's eyes, the snake dissolved into a black and red tattoo. The palm of his hand was stained with the ferocious gate of the serpent's mouth as if only moments before a strike with its tongue back, its eyes focusing forward, and its two needled fangs pulled up and back to make room for its prey. The wounds the snake created and forced itself into and out of cauterized and sealed before his eyes with all the sophistication of a branding iron, including the sound of sizzling skin and the escape of white smoke from burned flesh; it was a smell that instantly brought back the memories of the tormented bodies in hell.

Curtis continued to watch as his swollen and stretched skin flattened and the snake tattoo finished imprinting into his skin, starting at the top of his forearm and moving down to his wrist and onto his palm. He slowly, gradually twisted his wrist and arm, first clockwise and then counter clockwise. It felt heavy and unbalanced as though it was still off-centered by the weight of the snake. He stared at his new scars and tattoos like someone staring at the clock just minutes before the alarm is set to go off, trying to calculate how much time before the peaceful night officially ends and the curse of the day begins. Curtis broke the lock of his gaze from his arm and looked up at Satan.

The Seraphim's eyes were glistening black pools, and his face was frozen in erotic anticipation with all ten inches of his swollen member fully erect and displayed in front of him.

Curtis didn't give a shit about the boner, but he felt a bubbling, a kind of effervescence taking place within the flesh of his arm. Then he saw the black lines begin to travel up his veins. He slowly, sluggishly, reached his left hand over and rubbed them. They burned as they inched up his arm as though he had received a transfusion of battery acid. Now a new sensation hit him when he began to hear distant voices, cries, and screams. The voices got louder and the screams became clearer and more defined. Then Curtis heard gunshots. As the black sludge travelled further up his arm and towards his shoulder, he heard the screams of a woman and the laughter of a man, no – men. Then he saw them in a vision. He was floating above them. Two men were gang raping a young teenage girl behind a truck, a green army personnel carrier, to be more precise. He watched them take pleasure in pinning her down in the dirt, punching her in the face, forcing her legs apart, and forcing themselves into her. Curtis felt their pleasure, and their adrenaline. He read their corrupt minds. He heard one of them say they didn't need to pull out because she was already pregnant. There was something familiar about her. Gradually, Curtis recognized the bleeding young girl: she was the one from his *remembering*, the one separated from her family as they were murdered and left to rot in a ditch. Then he saw the movement of the truck and heard the unloading of more victims from the back of the carrier. Still floating above the scene, he was forced to watch as they continued to rape and beat the girl.

There was more to this vision, a deeper, underlining familiarity to the young woman. Curtis could hear other screams, other torments funneling in. It was unrelated to the view in front of him; somehow he knew atrocities, crimes against humanity, against nature, and against God himself were happening right now in the present – all over the world. As the black lines entered Curtis's chest, he found he cared less about them. In fact, he wanted to hear more of them. As he strained his ears listening, the vile acts and evil thoughts actually made him feel more powerful. He could see the world was fucked up and he was beginning to like it. He felt the satanic acid enter his heart and immediately begin its course through his body. He watched the two men continue to rape the woman and he wanted to join them. He heard more shots fired from the extermination squads behind him and wished he could have pulled the trigger – at least once. He inspected the blackening of his nails on his left hand and felt a corrosive coating darkening his eyes.

Then, in the animalistic orgy of the forced sex scene playing out in front of him, he heard the Yugoslavian guard comment about how Hungarian pussy was tighter than pussy from his own village.

What did he say? Curtis asked himself, his small bit of humanity hung onto the soldier's last phrase. The brutalized young woman was familiar to him, but how? Lucifer watched the small, almost imperceptible hiccup in Curtis's posture. The transformation within Curtis's eyes had stopped – perhaps temporarily – but he needed this hybrid. A human/Cherubim/Seraphim warrior would make an incredible lieutenant. He must finish the corruption. Lucifer unsheathed his sword and held it firmly in his hand, debating whether or not to give up his celestial weapon, reconsidering – perhaps – the incredible investment in his prodigy: a fantastic ally certainly, or an extraordinary foe. Lucifer read the apothegm scripted on the side. He knew the sword could never be used against him – directly – but that would also leave him defenseless from an angelic attack, at least until he formed a new one.

But then Curtis blinked again and took a step backwards. He couldn't shake the inescapable familiarity of the teenage girl. He watched as she gave up as the next man climbed on top of her. Her face, now calm and blank, stared at him. Curtis knew she was seeing him right now, looking at him. This chilled the lust that was growing in him. It slowed his rage.

As the man on top of her repositioned himself, she placed a gentle hand onto her belly and whispered, "Please, God, keep my Curtis safe."

Curtis didn't just feel his heart skip a beat, he felt it stop. He stared into the eyes of the young woman and now fully realized who she was. Lucifer watched the dramatic change hit Curtis and decided now was the time to take his warrior. He shoved the handle of his sword into Curtis's tattooed palm. The connection of the Seraphim's sword to Curtis's hand instantly fused the weapon to Curtis's soul. With the connection he heard all the atrocities of the world come down on him. The weight of the pain and suffering was too much, too heavy. Curtis collapsed to his knees and screamed out loud in agony. The faces, the tears, the hate flooded his thoughts, but this time it didn't penetrate him. The eyes and words of the young woman – his mother – shielded him.

Satan looked down at Curtis, not sure what to make of him. "Get up and rise... Prince," Lucifer said in triumph.

Curtis continued to scream, crumpled onto his knees, the sword heavy in his hand. His mind and soul were besieged by the voices and images of all the evil deeds committed throughout human history.

CHAPTER THIRTY

Ireland

The chartered bus from Dublin's International Airport to the village of Bushmills was a lack luster trip of five hours. The narrow back country roads and *actual* sheep crossings made it feel a lot longer.

But now, at 8:30 p.m., Vivica stretched out her legs on her king-sized, pillow-topped, four-poster canopy bed and ordered some room service. It wasn't often that she got to treat herself like a queen, but for the next few days she was going to enjoy what the hotel had to offer.

An impressive wind was blowing off the Atlantic Ocean, crashing large waves into the hexagonal stone pillars, ledges, and cliffs that made up the Giant's Causeway, spraying large plumes of ocean water into the air. On Weir's Snout, a plateau 100 meters above the Atlantic, Jennifer Leary was dressed in her traditional hooded robe. Using her athame she scratched out a six meter long pentagram into the thick sod and enclosed the knife within a circle. When the circle was complete she spread a thick paste of tea tree oil, beeswax, and salt from the Dead Sea into the engraved channels; the salt purified and consecrated the circle while the paste prevented the salt from being blown away in the breeze. Finally, Jennifer placed a lit candle lantern at each of the five points and she sat herself down in the penta-center with her athame and wand and began chanting the Summoning Spell:

Great Father hear us
Great Father near to us
Great Father come to us
Baal, Hecate open your gate
Isis, Selket, Nergal, Shamash
I call upon your powers
A bridge we ask

Open the gate from your world to ours
Open the gate from your world to ours
Open the gate from your world to ours

Magnus Pater audi nos
Magnus Pater prope nos
Magnus Pater venires ad nos
Baal, Hecate aperi januam
Isis, Selket, Nergal, Shamash
tuum invocamus
Morbi pontem
Aperite portam a saeculo nostro
Aperite portam a saeculo nostro
Aperite portam a saeculo nostro

CHAPTER THIRTY-ONE

knock, knock, knock
"Room Service!"

"That was quick," Vivica said to herself, "I'm starving." Shuffling across her large bed and landing heavy on her feet revealed how exhausted she really was. "Coming!" she said out loud to the door and to the room attendant on the other side of it as she forced her body to keep moving. "After this I am going to be dead to the world," she said as she pleasantly opened the door, anticipating the culinary pleasures of the five star hotel. Instead of the professionally tailored uniform of a hotel attendant, Vivica faced a man wearing black combat cargo pants and a black windbreaker with a NIKE ball cap.

"You've got that right," Joshua Goldstein said in his strong eastern accent. He stepped into the doorway and landed his fist squarely onto Vivica's jaw and upper lip. The solid punch launched Vivica on her backside deep into her room. Joshua closed the door behind him and dropped a duffle bag at Vivica's feet.

Pain and blood flooded Vivica's mouth as she stared at the ceiling in confusion. Her room spiraled and blinked in and out around her. Even if she wasn't caught completely off guard, she would have never in her life handled a blow like that. One time she got a slap in the face from a young female student who didn't believe she deserved the grade Vivica gave her for her report on Egyptian sandstone. This hit didn't even compare to that. Not fully registering the situation, Vivica tried to sit up and confront the bus boy.

"What the fu…?" Vivica slurred, clutching her jaw. "Ahhh…" she moaned in pain.

"Shut up or I strike you again."

Vivica looked down and saw blood on her hand. She immediately scrambled blindly backwards until she crashed into the solid oak bed frame.

"My purse is right there," she slurred pointing over to the night stand. Blood ran freely from her mouth and her neck screamed at her in pain. "Take whatever you want."

"Oh, I will, Vivica," Joshua said calmly and started to empty the bag. Vivica watched in horror as Joshua pulled out two neatly tied bundles of rope.

Oh my god he's going to rape me.

Then Joshua pulled out a grey tarpaulin.

He is going to rape and kill me. "Why are you doing this? Who are you? I don't even know you."

Vivica's panicked mind searched for any past connection with the man's face. There was none.

"I need you to shut fuck up now," he demanded in his broken English "your voice is bothering me. We need to go for a small ride down the road. We can do this easy way – you clean yourself up we walk out back door, or we do it hard way." Joshua pulled out a small, rectangular tin box about the same size as a pencil case from the duffle bag.

"No!" Vivica said, quiet at first and then again a little louder. The expression on her face was like that of a trapped animal. Frantically, she grabbed at the bed comforter behind her and pulled herself to her feet. The pain in her jaw and neck were gone as her body pumped with adrenaline. Her mind searched for some strategy for escape.

I need out of here.

The surest exit was the door to the hallway, but the stranger stood between them. The window...

Vivica quickly looked behind her over the bed at the window. Thick and heavy curtains hid the glass and metal frame structure somewhere behind them.

Joshua followed her eyes. *It's always the hard way.*

I will have to dive through the center where the curtains meet, she thought thinly, her mind still racing with panic. *Can't run around the bed; he will catch me for sure.*

Vivica turned and launched herself onto the massive bed. Just minutes earlier she had used the enormous divan built for royalty to escape the hectic modern world. It had been a luxurious getaway all on its own, but now it was a 6x6 barrier with mammoth pillows and a plush comforter.

Joshua pounced with lightning speed onto the bed as his own adrenaline pumped. He leaped a little too high and unintentionally connected his head mid-flight with the artistically carved and decorated wooden canopy beam. The unexpected hit stopped him for a moment in his tracks, but then he promptly refocused on his target.

The abrupt *crack* from behind caused Vivica to hastily look over her shoulder; on the bed the stranger stood swaying and blinking. She quickly donkey-kicked behind her, landing her heel exactly on his left knee, which buckled his leg backwards. Squirming and kicking her way across the quicksand-like bed, her fingers grasped the edge of the mattress and she pulled herself forward.

When Vivica's heel connected with Joshua's left knee, it forced his leg to bend unnaturally backwards. If it wasn't for the tread of Joshua's boot slipping on the bed spread, it might have possibly broken his leg and compromised the mission, something the KACH or Chavah wouldn't like. The sobering pain, however, brought him back to the present and he saw that the bitch was getting away. Joshua leaped again and stabbed a needle and syringe into Vivica's back between her shoulder blades and just right of her spine.

"Help!" Vivica screamed, mostly in vain, as Joshua shoved her face into the fabric of the bed.

Fighting ravenously for both air and escape, Vivica could feel the needle's tip scraping the muscle and bone deep in her back.

Joshua had to move fast and press down the plunger before she broke off the needle. The syringe contained a combination of sodium thiopental and diazepam. Sodium thiopental or sodium pentothal has been misrepresented by Hollywood as a truth serum, but rather than releasing one's inhibitions and exposing all secrets, it only depresses the central nervous system and suppresses muscle function; it's a fast-acting but short-lasting tranquilizer. When added with Ketamine (Diazepam), a little goes a long way. The injection should knock Vivica out for about two hours or maybe more for a person of her size.

With one hand forcing Vivica's face into the sheets and the other her right arm, Joshua had to lean on the plunger and press it down with his chest.

Unable to breath, scream or even move, Vivica felt a cold sensation spread through her back. She couldn't tell if she was drugged or dying from suffocation – or perhaps both – but her body slowly gave in. Her own muscles mutinied against her and then gave up altogether. Finally, her body succumbed to blackness.

Once Joshua felt Vivica's body go limp, he sat up behind her and waited to see if she was playing possum. After several seconds, when he believed she was significantly tranquilized, he grabbed her by the hair and rotated her head so she could breath. Bright red blood smeared the comforter where her face had been pressed and continued to trickle from her lips.

He climbed backwards off of the bed, his leg throbbing, and moved the coffee table and a large chair to open up the area and make space for the tarp. He forced his breathing under control and then called down to the reception desk to cancel Vivica's room service. *No need to have them walking in at the wrong time.*

Joshua reached across the bed, grabbed Vivica by the ankles, and pulled her to the side of the bed where he was standing. The needle and syringe, still embedded into her back, bobbed and swayed in the air. He plucked out the syringe and tossed it on the bed beside her. He then hoisted her petite frame down onto the tarpaulin, secured her hands and feet with one of the ropes, and tied the tarp closed with the other.

Finally, after retrieving the tin case that held the solution plus several spare syringes, and making sure he picked up any other items that fell out of his bag, he did a quick check of the hallway. *Empty.*

Joshua flung Vivica's cocooned body over his shoulder, grabbed his bag and exited out the door. Twenty minutes later, they pulled up to Weir's Snout plateau in his rented Range Rover. The wind had died down considerably and a clear night sky set the canvas for a full, bright moon. In the distance, the ocean still sounded angry.

Joshua didn't know what to expect when his GPS notified him he had reached his destination, but a robed figure kneeling and chanting in the centre of a twenty foot pentagram would have not – in a thousand years – been one of them. Curious, even interested, but undaunted, Joshua placed the vehicle in PARK and left it running with the headlamps illuminating the site – a lesson he learned during an operation back in his earlier years. As he cracked the door to step out of the vehicle, the smell of apple blossoms filled his nostrils. Chavah, still dressed in the same black outfit as when he first met Joshua in Hebron, stood beside the Rover.

"Fuck!" Joshua blurted, startled by his sudden appearance. "Where did you come from?"

"You brought the woman?" Chavah questioned, uninterested in Joshua's own questioning.

"She's in back."

"Get her and bring her to the edge of the circle," Chavah demanded.

Joshua limped over to the back of the SUV and lifted Vivica's still unconscious form onto his shoulder. She remained tied but she was no longer wrapped within the tarp.

"Are you injured?" Chavah asked, concern noticeable in his voice.

"The bitch almost broke my leg."

"But you are well? Your body must not get hurt," Chavah said, looking Joshua up and down.

"I'll be fine," he returned, feeling a bit uncomfortable with the large man's distress. At the circle, Joshua looked around at the large, carved out pentagram and again at the kneeling figure (which, up close, he could now tell was a woman) swinging a stick in her hand while she continued to chant and sway her body in a figure eight motion. The blade from a knife on the ground in front of her reflected the candle and the moonlight.

"Place her here in the grass," Chavah said, motioning down towards his feet.

Joshua slid Vivica's unconscious body off of his shoulder and carelessly dropped her onto the grassy plateau.

"Where are the weapons you promised me?" he asked impatiently.

"It's coming, son of David. You will get all that you have asked for and even more."

"When?" Joshua pushed further, zipping his wind breaker up to his chin. "It's cold here."

"In about two and a half hours. Go and wait in your vehicle."

Joshua looked around the desolate plateau. He heard the crashing waves but was unable to see exactly where the basalt cliff dropped off to the ocean. Then he looked back to the hooded witch doing… whatever the hell she was doing.

“This is messed up!” he exclaimed and returned to the comfort of the Range Rover.

CHAPTER THIRTY-TWO

"Get up!" Lucifer demanded, this time with annoyance and disappointment in his voice. "Get up or I will use your precious Charlie to motivate you."

Charlie's name struck a chord deep within Curtis. The thought of his daughter pierced the depth that was quickly becoming a tomb of despair. Her soft snores sliced through the screams of the damned. It pulled him out from the edge of Hades. Curtis closed his mouth and looked over at the golden sword that was now secured in his grasp. Strength pumped through him, unbelievable strength. The voices and screams stopped altogether as he stared at the sword. He reinforced his grip on the handle. It no longer felt heavy, but was light – feather light. It hummed, vibrated and pulsed with their combined energy. Beyond the sword he noticed the white feet and black nails of Lucifer.

Still kneeling, he raised his gaze to meet Satan's and hoped the determination behind his stare would drive home that he no longer feared the fallen angel.

"You go near her, and I will rid the world of the devil – for good."

Satan examined his new hybrid, trying quickly to read his thoughts, but he couldn't, which was unexpected – and not good. Gambling, he stood his ground against Curtis.

"You can't hurt me with my own sword," he said meekly. "You can not threaten me! I am the Angel of Light, the Lord of Darkness. I – I am Satan. I am Ha-Sata. I will kill... destroy everyone you hold dear. If you raise your voice to me again I will torture their souls for all eternity. I will..."

Curtis continued to stare into the black depths of Lucifer's eyes. Without saying a word, the Sword of Jophiel materialized in Curtis's left hand. Lucifer's voice stopped cold. He stared back at the human/Cherubim/Seraphim in astonishment. Curtis felt Lucifer falter, felt his astonishment, his shock.

"He... gave you *his* sword?" Lucifer questioned. "Jophiel gave...? You hold the sword of a Cherubim...? Impossible!" he said, the last part mostly to himself.

Curtis continued to stare defiantly. His eyes felt like they were on fire and they now blazed silver like pools of liquid mercury.

"My sword will not harm me human, and Jophiel's sword will not finish me. How dare you challenge me," Lucifer roared, his voice defensive and sharp.

Curtis lowered his gaze and shifted his eyes from his right hand to his left. Lucifer mistook the meaning of Curtis's gaze, believing his own threatening tone had curbed his dog. "Stand and I will forget your insubordination, human."

Curtis remained kneeling and stared at his swords. Then he did something that had never – in the eternity of all eternities – been done before. Curtis slammed both blades together. The energy of the divine weapons coming into contact with each other as they shared a link to the same soul exploded. The force blew the living room and dining room furniture out the windows. Lucifer and Curtis stayed as they were, unharmed, unmoved as the blast continued to blow out the walls and the ceiling of the house. It spread out at the speed of light, disintegrating the neighbourhood homes, apartments and office buildings across the harbor. The explosion cascaded through Nova Scotia, and then New Brunswick, Maine and New York, obliterating everything. As the ripple devastated the land, spreading out like an unstoppable nuclear shockwave, it was also projected out into space. It left the earth and plowed into the moon, sending its fine layers of dust out into the void like a drift of fresh snow. It carried on and collided with the sun, forcing the star's gaseous surface away from the impact, momentarily creating a fiery tear drop. In that first second, the hyper-divine blast tore through the entire solar system and affected every heavenly body. Within a fraction of the next second, the blast wave was sucked back, its devastation reversing. Like a movie rewinding, the sun, moon, buildings, bridges and trees were all righted back to their original state. Even the furniture within the Papp home was returned exactly as it was.

Except for Curtis.

Curtis used his own soul to melt the two swords into one. He knelt there at the feet of Lucifer now holding only one *black* sword. The blade of the new sword was now four feet long. Eight inches at the tip of the sword split and divided into two distinct blades, as if the blades themselves couldn't stand to be near each other. This new sword, a hybrid of the two, was no heavier than either one of its parents, which is to say it had no weight at all. But it hummed, loudly, and it discharged sparks and crackled with raw electricity. Curtis stared at the black rapier and so did Lucifer.

"What you created there is unnatural," Satan lectured. "It has *never* been done. It *should* have never been done."

Curtis looked up at the naked Seraphim and thought just one thought: *pathetic.*

Lucifer didn't read Curtis's thought as much as Curtis projected it to him. Satan reexamined the new being in front of him and took a step back. Curtis's aura was all over the spectrum. He radiated intensely, and then, like a vacuum, he sucked in all heat and life within close proximity. Lucifer took another step back. Curtis stood up and looked at the first fallen angel. Curtis felt physically larger than he did before, taller.

"You should leave; you're not welcome here," Curtis said, his tone flat and very threatening. The bubble that Lucifer created to isolate them inside of Curtis's house abrogated away like a breeze blowing away mist. Lucifer stared at Curtis with his mouth agape, and took another step backwards. His eyes were confused and questioning, never leaving Curtis. The end table that held the picture of Vivica slid to his right and the chesterfield slid to his left by an unseen force that made way for Lucifer's step. Curtis breathed hard and angry as he stared at the Seraphim; his sword was ready in his hand.

Although Curtis's head was swimming and the cells in his body were intoxicated with a truly supernatural power, he clearly identified the unmistakable look of fear in Satan's eyes.

The Jinn disconnected themselves from the shadows created by the hanging chandelier. Creeping out from under the dining table and chairs, they detached from their roost and in unison travelled toward the wall behind Lucifer. More shadows from under the recliner, chesterfield, coffee table, and every dark corner within the room broke free from their hidden nests that gave them existence and met with their brethren to form a dark door frame. Satan stepped back into the shadowy gateway. Dark silk fingers like the ones that had released him earlier when he entered into the room reached and re-embraced his pale skin. When the last tip of his flesh dissolved into the portal, the doorway blinked out of existence the way darkness collapses at the snap of a light switch.

Quickly, Curtis turned and bolted to the stairway, his sword no longer in his tattooed hand.

Eavery stood at the top of the stairs watching as Curtis charged up towards him. "What happened here?" he asked, jumping out of the way. "I couldn't sense you, or Charlie, or even this house. It was like you were gone."

Curtis barreled passed Eavery, stripping off his soiled clothes in the bathroom and hopping into a not yet warm but still cleansing shower. Curtis hardly registered Eavery in his home, let alone Eavery's questioning. His mind raced thinking about Charlie and Vivica.

When he shut off the water, Curtis slid the shower curtain open with a mere suggestion and movement of his hand. As he reached out for the towel it leaped into his hand from a meter away.

"Curtis, what happened here?" Eavery shouted from the other side of the door. Just then the bathroom door opened and Curtis shot out with a towel around his waist and still lost in his own dilemma.

Eavery saw the snake tattoo on Curtis's right arm, and as Curtis dashed by on the way to his bedroom, he saw the ghostly silhouette of a white wing coming out of his right shoulder blade.

"What have you done?" Eavery asked slowly, following his friend into the room. The fear and concern he had for his friend's safety only seconds ago became a numbing paralysis of his divine faculties at the realization of what had happened there.

"What have you become?"

This question from Eavery pierced the chaotic firestorm in Curtis's brain. He pulled a yellow t-shirt with the RCAF roundel on the front down over his head and turned to confront Eavery.

Curtis exhaled and tried to calm his thoughts. "I did what I had to do."

Eavery could barely recognize the man standing in front of him. His face, hair, and body was Curtis Papp, corporal in the Royal Canadian Air force, father to Charlie and husband to Vivica, but the soul that was now bound to the mortal flesh was not the same Curtis he met less than a week ago. That human soul was now fully replaced with a Nephilim soul. He could see specter wings: one black wing sprouting out of

Curtis's left side and one white wing sprouting out of Curtis's right side that had now coupled to his spirit and attached to his soul.

Curtis Papp had become a hybrid with elevated angelic DNA: a combination of divine Cherubim and ultra-divine Seraphim encapsulated within a human host.

Eavery could sense the death rapier secured invisibly (even to his eyes) to the snake tattoo of his right arm.

Curtis read the intimidation, conflict, and fear in Eavery. He hadn't lost so much of his humanity that he couldn't sense his friend's discomfort; he could and it bothered him. He might not be the same *old* Curtis, but he wasn't Frankenstein's monster bent on wreaking havoc and destruction on the innocent either, only on those who wanted to hurt his family.

"Eavery," Curtis said and reached out to console his friend.

Irrational or not, fear pulled Eavery away, causing Curtis's hand to brush the air where Eavery's shoulder once was.

Knowing that he caused his friend fear for his own safety hurt Curtis, but unfortunately now wasn't the time to make amends. Curtis reached into his closet for an old pair of combat boots, pulled them on, and then walked into Charlie's room.

"Peanut, time to get up," he said softly, brushing the hair that framed her tiny face with his hand.

"Daddy," Charlie said, rubbing her eyes and looking up at him, "you look different. You've changed."

"Yeah, so I've heard. Come on kiddo, we've gotta go."

"Are we going to get mommy?" she asked, sitting up. Her right hand reached for the pink blanket she always slept with.

Putting slippers onto her feet he replied, “Yes we are.”

“It’s about time,” she smiled. “You have wings too, just like your bird friend.”

Curtis hoisted Charlie up into his arms.

“Are we going to fly there?”

“Something like that.”

In a flash of light the room was empty.

CHAPTER THIRTY-THREE

Joshua Goldstein sat impatiently in the Range Rover waiting for the headlights of the cargo truck that was supposed to deliver his "miracle" weapons so he could free Israel and Palestine from all the non-Jews and reclaim the Holy Land. When the Rover's dashboard clock displayed 11:55 PM, he had reached the end of his patience. Just then, a yellow and orange glowing cloud formed and churned high above the plateau.

"Finally – something's happening!" he said aloud in the cab.

Vivica's head pounded as she sat quietly in the thick, damp grass. Her muscles, still under the influence from the injection, felt heavy. Combined with the exposure to the plateau's open environment, a depressing coldness settled deep into her core.

"Do not fear, child," Chavah said, walking around into her view. "It is not you we want."

"Then why am I here?" Vivica yelled, panic and physical stress controlling the volume of her voice. "I've been punched, drugged, and kidnapped. I don't even know you people."

"It is your daughter we want – and she is on her way."

"Charlie?" A whole other level of dread filled Vivica at the thought of anyone harming her child. *How do they know Charlie? Why would they want her?*

Vivica looked over at the chanting figure and realized she was the woman Vivica had met in the airport. Jennifer chanted endlessly on the ground as if possessed, and then up to the cloud formation that seemed to unnaturally appear and suspend itself above them. It was an eerie sight, like something out of a movie. Vivica thought, if only Jennifer would stop chanting, then maybe that would bring some perspective to what is happening to me. But the whole event felt more like a dream – a nightmare – than like reality.

Jennifer Leary stopped chanting, and for a second the plateau was dead quiet. Then her arms shot out, her head flung back, and she screamed as brilliant beams of white light blasted from her eyes and mouth into the supernatural cloud above them. The rays of light bellowed out a sound like the deep roar of a blast furnace.

"The time has come; he is finally here," Chavah said, his eyes sparkling. In front of Vivica, white and pink apple blossoms fell from the large man like dead skin crumbling off an ancient Egyptian mummy. But instead of an exposed skeleton of a long gone pharaoh, there stood a vibrant and beautiful woman dressed in an elegant pink and white Abaya and hijab.

"Oh my God!" Vivica whispered in disbelief.

"What... is going on here?" Joshua asked himself inside the Range Rover, also stunned at what he was seeing. Joshua climbed out of the vehicle and limped over to Vivica and the strange woman, unsuccessfully trying to comprehend the sight unfolding before him.

"Ah, good son of David, hold the woman and I will finish the gateway for my husband's return."

Joshua obediently grabbed Vivica by the arms and pulled her to her feet, all the while staring at the woman who used to be Chavah.

"What happened to the man, Chavah?" Joshua asked his voice barely perceptible above the howling beams.

"We are one and the same. I find his appearance can sometimes be more persuasive. Her husband and child will soon be here, so you must make sure she does not escape."

Joshua eyed Eve both cautiously and suspiciously as he weaved one arm in between Vivica's and wrapped the other around her neck as though he was using her as a human shield, which is what he was prepared to do anyway, if necessary. Eve lifted the glass from one of the candles and kicked it over into the wax. The wax melted slowly at first but then the tea tree oil ignited. In a chain reaction, the fire spread along the outline of the pentagram. Once the fire looped around and completed the circle, it finished the link of the Jacob's Ladder.

The light from the burning wax stretched itself skyward like a golden cylinder until it reached the ominous cloud, trapping the pentagram and Jennifer Leary inside of it. Lightning exploded downwards from the heavenly contact point, blasting and assaulting the exposed stone along the edge of the carved out circle. Fried mud, grass, and broken bits of basalt stone sprayed Joshua, Vivica and Eve. Instinctively, Joshua moved back from the violent lightning storm and pulled Vivica with him. Eve, on the contrary, stood her ground just centimeters from the unrelenting barrage. Charged by the lightning, the high iron content within the basalt stone liquefied and formed a molten ring. When the last bit of the ring fused together, the lightning stopped; the thunder echoed and rolled off the cliffs and out through the country side.

Eve's face glowed with her own internal lightning. Her heart pumped wildly knowing that very soon she would once again hold the first man she ever loved. They had been apart for thousands of years, and dozens of times in the past she had tried to reunite them, but tonight the Fates had weaved in her favour. *Tonight*, she thought, *I will finally succeed. Tonight Adam and Eve will be together again. Tonight will be the second coming of the First One and the second creation of the Garden of Eden.*

"Joshua, we need to get out of here," Vivica whispered as she stared at Eve. "She's going to kill us both."

"I'm not going to die, but you might. I have a deal with... them."

"You have a deal with her or the big biker guy she used to be? Look around you," Vivica said, trying not to raise her voice, but panic was close to overcoming her. "This isn't natural. It isn't even supernatural... this is biblical. That woman in the circle has beams of light shooting out of her face, Joshua. There is a golden cloud hovering above us and a lightning storm just formed a perfect iron ring from the FUCKING GROUND! People who see this kind of shit never walk away from it," Vivica shrieked.

As if snapping out of some kind of trance, Joshua looked around the scene with fresh eyes. Technically, he hadn't missed all that had just happened, but until now it never impacted him; it was somehow – filtered. Now the filter was off and he needed to get his ass out of there, and fast. *Forget the weapons!* he thought. *He/she never did say what it was anyway, never even showed me a hint of it.* Without saying a word, Joshua shoved Vivica away from him. With her arms and feet were still bound by the rope, she fell face first onto her stomach.

"Don't leave me here! Take me with you!" she yelled after him, unfazed by the impact.

Chavah doesn't need me anymore; she has the woman, Joshua thought to himself as he dashed for the idling Range Rover; its headlamps blinded him. He reached for the door handle as he hurried around the 4x4, anxious to get off the plateau, and off the damp island, and back to the warm Mediterranean. His fingers were stopped just short of the metal by Eve's vice-like grasp on his wrist.

"You can't go anywhere, Joshua Ephram Goldstein. I need you... *he* needs you," Eve said, her eyes shifting from Joshua's eyes to the cloud above them.

"Who is *he*?"

The longing smile of a lover evident on Eve's face. Just the thought of him warmed the deep coldness that had settled into her over the millennia.

"Adam, my husband, of course. His soul sits there waiting," she turned her head more and looked up at the cloud. "Soon we will be together again. We will recreate Eden – *our* Heaven on Earth, this time for all eternity."

Joshua swallowed hard. This woman was undoubtedly psychotic, but the light show and glowing cloud tilted his fear in her favour.

"Why does he need me? You have girl."

"The woman is to get the Nephilim here. He has the child that I need. But my husband's soul needs a vessel to return to – and it must be a true son from the line of David. After all, God's chosen people were *our* children."

"You want me for what?" Joshua asked as he pulled and jerked his hand out from Eve's seemingly fragile clutch, but she didn't move – not even a little. He should have easily been able to toss her small frame aside like he had done dozens of times with men larger, heavier, and better armed than himself. But he couldn't. Either she had somehow hypnotized him and was now manipulating him or… she actually was Eve, the wife of Adam and the sacred matriarch of mankind.

"Come, Joshua, do not challenge me. Stand by me when your father's father comes back to this world. A new bible is being written; a new Genesis is taking place. Your selfless sacrifice will ensure your name will forever live on. In the *re*-beginning, Joshua Ephram Goldstein created man…"

Eve's spellbound words flowed through Joshua like an ancient siren drawing an unsuspecting ship closer to hidden shoals. She used his pride and quest for immortality (that all men have) as the bait to lure him back to the circle.

CHAPTER THIRTY- FOUR

Vivica lay on her side and watched how Eve held the thug's wrist and then guided him around like an obedient dog. The panic and fear that was very evident in his face only moments ago was replaced with a blank stare. He had either been fully bewitched by the woman or he finally gave in to her – Vivica wasn't sure which. But Vivica also overheard the woman say she was a pawn to get a 'nephilim – something' here and a child. Looking back at the idling Range Rover, she knew that was her only way out. With her hands tied behind her back and her feet still bound together, she wasn't able to drive, but there must be something sharp in the back of the truck – in his duffle bag.

With Eve's attention focused on the zombified Joshua, Vivica calculated that now would be her best chance to work her way over to the vehicle undetected. She clumsily and painfully rolled herself toward the Rover. The uneven ground with large clumps of thick grass made the trek slow and exhausting, but every roll away from the circle was that much closer to freedom. Unfortunately for Vivica, Eve was all too aware of what she was doing.

"Now, what are you trying to do, my dear?" Eve asked in a very motherly, non-threatening manner. To Vivica, this made Eve sound even more sinister.

Eve raised the palm of her hand up; Vivica, in turn, rose up onto her feet. As Eve rotated her wrist, Vivica also rotated until the two women were facing each other.

"Come to me, child," Eve softly said and folded her fingers into her palm. As if suspended by invisible cables, Vivica felt her body being physically pulled back toward the circle, losing all the ground she had just made and more as she came face to face with Eve.

"You can't leave until your husband and daughter come to rescue you."

Curtis and Charlie are coming here? A new kind of panic and dread blossomed in Vivica.

Eve continued, "The ancient spirit of the Táltos that has reincarnated itself as your daughter is the sacrifice I need to break the boundary between the Nether World and this one. Her sacrifice will free my husband and your daughter's name will live on forever in the new Bible, as will yours, I promise."

"I don't give a fuck about your new Bible… or your husband. I am not going to let you murder Charlie in this… cult ritual." Vivica pulled against the ropes with everything she had. Her muscles fought against the knots and the drugs that were still in her system. "I am going to rip your face off!"

"Vivica, I understand your loss. I too lost a child, a son, and that pain never goes away. But I offer you paradise in the new Eden, or you can suffer an eternity in limbo. All those that die after the formation of Eden will be trapped; the gates to Heaven and Hell will be closed forever."

Eve casually twirled her forefinger and Vivica swung upside down; her hair rested on the ground. Blood rushed to her head. Her jaw and lips throbbed and began bleeding again from the pressure.

"Genevieve Cynthia Leary," Eve said, turning her attention back to the pentagram. "It is time to pick up your knife."

Jennifer Leary was trapped within her own rapidly decaying body. The beams of light blasting out of her eyes and mouth were literally dissolving her and pulling her fragments into the air along the beam, creating the thin but physical steps of the ladder.

Her long red hair had already fallen out and the skin on her emaciated, sunken face was peeling back. She was burning from the massive energy she was exuding. How did she get here? She should have been celebrating in Egypt with Liam. She knew now that she would never see him again. For some reason, Raphael had tricked her, betrayed her, and used her. Doing as she was told, her eyes locked onto the cloud; the beams of light never veered from their mark as Jennifer blindly reached down in front of her and grabbed her knife. The athame was cold and solid in her withered fingers.

"Now, daughter of Raphael, your name will live on for eternity. Open the gate."

Jennifer raised the blade of her athame and pressed the tip to her cheek. Even upside down with blood pounding in her head, Vivica watched in horror.

"Jennifer, what are you doing? Put the knife down. What are you doing to her? No, Jennifer, DON'T!"

Unable to control her own movements, Jennifer pierced her cheek with the tip of the blade. Pushing the knife inward, her thin, tissue-paper-like skin gave way easily. Radiant light shot out from the wound around the steel edges. Almost lost in the roar of the escaping beam, Vivica could hear Jennifer moan. Tears could no longer form from the glowing cavities that once held her eyes, but Vivica knew Jennifer was crying. Somewhere inside that tortured corpse, that poor woman could feel the pain of the knife slicing through her skin. The cheek fully opened, adding twice the amount of luminous light into the sky. Jennifer continued on and sliced open the other cheek. With her last breath, she finally screamed out loud as the new, greater beam dissolved the remaining tissue and bones within her face, creating one large shaft of light. What was left of Jennifer Leary's body collapsed in the center of the circle. Her cloak flopped and rolled around as the remainder of her corpse finished the ladder. Pleased with her own progress, Eve twirled her forefinger again and righted Vivica.

"There, is that better, child?" Eve asked, and with her hand she wiped away some of the blood that had trailed down Vivica's cheek and around the curve of her eye and accumulated in the delicate hairs of her brow.

"Let's try to look our best for his arrival, shall we?"

Repulsed at being touched by Eve, Vivica wanted to pull away but then thought better of it.

Eve released Joshua's wrist and ordered him to place his statuette into his hand. "Now hold it into the circle."

The ancient sandstone figurine bounced and danced on his trembling hand. As his hand entered the light produced by the iron ring, the eyes of the gargoyle began to glow brightly.

"That's it, that's it. Hold it there," Eve said excitedly. "Come to me, my love," she shouted up into the cloud.

"Come to me, Adam." She smiled at the thought of thousands of years of longing and loneliness coming to an end.

A man's bare foot broke free from the paranormal cloud and stepped down on the top rung of the ladder. Eve wept and vibrated with emotion at the first sight of her husband. Then his other foot broke free and slowly, with each step down, Adam materialized from the gateway of the Nether World. Almost hyperventilating, Eve trembled as he continued downward.

In a blinding flash of light, Curtis, with Charlie in his arms, appeared on the plateau. He never gave much thought to what he was expecting to see when he left his house, but a naked man walking down the steps of a transportal doorway enclosed in a bright golden shield on top of a grassy plateau was not it.

"Mommy!" Charlie yelled out seeing Vivica standing next to Eve.

Quickly, Curtis looked over and saw Vivica standing next to the two strangers. His heart fell when he saw dried blood smeared across her mouth and what appeared to be fresh blood streaming down from her eye.

"Charlie! Curtis! Get out of here! It's a trap!" Vivica screamed, the horror of losing her family was playing out as planned and she was helpless to stop it.

Eve pulled her focus from her husband to her new visitors. "Ah, you're here. Right on time," Eve said, giving Vivica a small shove and pushing her to the ground.

"Come to me, child," Eve said to Charlie, ignoring Curtis.

Curtis held tightly onto his daughter. Examining the scene, he looked at Joshua standing motionless with his hand in the golden zone, and then at Eve, and finally back at Vivica sitting in the grass with her arms and feet tied by ropes.

"Eve, let my wife go," Curtis demanded. "This is between you and me."

"She wants Charlie," Vivica shouted. "She wants to *sacrifice* her."

Curtis glanced at Charlie and then at Eve. This whole time he believed he was the sacrifice. And with his new gifts he thought he would walk in, take Vivica, and walk out. *If Satan is afraid of me*, he thought, *then no one can stop me, right?* He had unknowingly brought Charlie into the lion's den, which was the lion's plan all along.

Eve watched the realization in Curtis's eyes. Everything was going as planned. "The two of you were destined for tonight. For centuries I have waited for another Táltos to walk the Earth, and then centuries more for one this young," Eve said.

Her face changed to Lindsey Hilroy, the civilian liaison that briefed Curtis for his trip to Israel. "You had to be elevated, Curtis." Then her face and voice changed again to David Chodosh, the young Israeli airman that drove him to Nevatim. "As you changed, Charlie changed. Her ancient spirit had to be awakened. She too had to be elevated; she is the only sacrifice powerful enough to merge my husband's soul into a descendant of David."

Did Eavery know about all of this? Was this part of his plan too?

"It took some planning, Curtis," Eve continued. "But it all worked out in the end. I even had to intervene with that Hungarian cult. Apparently they had a mole in your little luncheon group."

Mole? Curtis thought. *Who could that be? Who would turn on their own kind?*

Eve changed back to herself and continued, "They picked up Brent Martin quickly after he *changed*, and instead of killing him and his family right then, they used him to find out who everyone in your group was. Eventually they finished off his wife and child but on that rainy Saturday morning, I had to intervene by nudging the steering wheel of that white van at the last second, killing Brent instead of you." Eve paused to let the news sink in. "Yes, Curtis, you and Charlie were the targets that day. The two of you were supposed to have been killed in front of the library. You see, I gave you and Charlie a few more days together. I believe in family, and now it is time I am reunited with mine."

"Come to me Charlie Asia Papp," Eve said with her hand extended out. "Come to me child."

Curtis could feel Eve's power broadcasting off of her toward them; he felt the lure even though it was directed at Charlie. The young four year old squinted and studied Eve, and then very plainly returned, "That doesn't work on me."

Eve's tender smile slid off her face and she transformed her motherly expression into a dark scowl. Charlie's defiance was the push that Curtis needed.

"Vivica!" Curtis focused his energy and thrust out his arm (like he did the day earlier when he tried to grab the pear). Today he was more powerful, thanks to Lucifer. *Hopefully I will have better luck with my wife than I had with the fruit.* Holding Charlie in his left arm, her legs wrapped around his waist and resting on his hip, Curtis felt his energy explode down his right arm and out the tips of his fingers and travel across the ten meter gap to Vivica. Even at that distance he knew her; he recognized her soul. He pulled her and drew her to him.

CHAPTER THIRTY-FIVE

Vivica felt something very odd. Sitting with her rump in the grass thirty feet away from Curtis and Charlie, she swore she could feel Curtis caressing her ankles. She didn't know how she *knew* it was Curtis – maybe because he was standing there with his hand reaching out to her – but she could *feel* him. Then she moved. Still sitting with her feet tied and hands bound behind her back, she started to slide forward. Just a few centimeters at first, and then she lurched a meter and landed heavy again on the ground. Startled by the quick jerk and harsh drop, Vivica was confused by what was happening. She knew Eve somehow moved her and even turned her upside down without ever touching her, but did Curtis also possess this mystical ability? She always considered herself a rational person; she was, after all, a professor at an Ivy League university. But what she had seen in the last hour had created within her a whole new respect for the supernatural, and perhaps even for the spiritual. Either she'd had some kind of mental breakdown while she was resting in her hotel room and this "experience" was only a delusional episode – which was the most likely reasoning and (believe it or not) the most comforting – or she was healthy, this was really happening and ancient religions and magic are real, a stairway to Heaven materialized from thin air, Curtis and Charlie just "popped" onto the Irish plateau in a flash of light, and now Curtis was telekinetically dragging her across the grass. This meant the world that Vivica was comfortable with was fucked.

Eve watched Vivica hop towards Curtis. She felt Curtis's energy and knew he was pulling her. But there was no way this night was going to end any differently than the way she had planned. As Vivica was pulled another meter, Eve reached out again with her own ability and caught Vivica in mid-air.

Vivica waited for the heavy drop, and when it didn't happen she looked down and realized she was floating. An invisible force grasped her ankles, pulling her towards her family, but now the energy she knew was Eve's was pulling her back to the circle, slowly overpowering her husband.

A smile returned to Eve's mouth as she felt Vivica coming back her way. She didn't hate the Papps. She wasn't trying to destroy them. On the contrary, she loved them. All the people on earth were her children, and she felt that connection. But after tens of thousands of years of heartache and loneliness she was now only moments away from holding her Adam. Their sacrifice tonight would live on forever in the new Bible; she would guarantee it. She knew the sacrifice must happen tonight. It was now the 21st of June; the solstice had begun and all the cosmic alignments were perfect.

Adam descended from the last step of Jacob's Ladder onto the consecrated ground within the circle. Although he was still a spirit without a body, his soul looked very solid, and very real. Naked, he stood next to the burning mound that used to be Jennifer Leary. He curled his toes into the grass, feeling it again after countless years away from the physical world. Eve's eyes were fixed on her husband. With her heart pounding, she was in awe at the miracle that was unfolding: *the rebirth of the First One.*

CHAPTER THIRTY-SIX

Joshua Goldstein changed his mind; this wasn't the plan. He was promised a secret weapon to save Israel and sacrificing himself wasn't part of the equation. His own pride got him to this place and Eve's unholy magic had trapped him here. He was a prisoner within his own body. Eve's words controlled him like a puppet; they played with his self-discipline until finally they didn't play at all and just moved him as she wished. Unable to budge a single muscle, his hand held the stone statuette of Adam four feet above the iron ring. It was the only break in the sacred circle and the only connection between his world and the supernatural plane where Adam currently existed. He now instinctively knew once Adam placed his own hand on top of the talisman their souls would merge, and he would either be possessed by Adam's spirit or forever roam the Nether World in his stead. In either scenario, the First One would soon have his body. His life started to play out in front of him. He was born in a community outpost created by a powerful government trying to spread its Jewish people throughout the Palestinian countryside. He remembered that as a young child, he was one of only a handful of children in a segregated Hebrew school within a dominantly Arab neighbourhood and had to endure the chastising stares and the threats. He was even spit on by Muslim strangers who were as much afraid of his kind as he was afraid of them. It wasn't hard to see the politics of the game, even at his age. Propaganda flowed out from both communities as to who was the rightful heir to the Holy Land. From birth he was brainwashed to believe it was his country for his people – everyone else must either get out, or succumb to second citizenry.

As Joshua got older the propaganda grew and so did the settlements. Now it was his turn to do the spitting and to make the threats. But the small skirmishes back and forth were becoming pointless. He needed a powerful weapon to end this battle, and before tonight he would have done anything for it.

But now, he had changed his mind; this wasn't part of the plan. The lure of an all powerful weapon, and of course his own pride, got him to where he is now. Joshua Goldstein intuitively knew that tonight was not going to end in his favour.

Curtis watched Adam step upon the grass and he could tell Eve was distracted by him. He knew this was his only chance. With his arm still stretched out, he thought about holding his wife again. He thought about the many years they would still have together, would still share together, and he pulled harder, hoping it wasn't going to result in a physical tug-of-war with Eve that ended up with Vivica's body getting hurt, or worse – torn apart – while he was trying to save her. He didn't dare rush over to her and bring Charlie closer to Eve.

Charlie, my little baby girl with incredible, unique gifts.

Curtis turned to Charlie hanging off of his side. "Charlie, you gotta help me. I need to pull mommy over to us."

"Okay, Daddy," Charlie said and placed her small hand onto Curtis' extended arm. She closed her eyes and began humming a soft melody. The stressed look on her young face softened.

Immediately, Curtis could feel the warmth of her hand on his bare skin. Her soft voice filled his head and the air around them. The warm touch spread down his arm and up his shoulder and continued to wash over him like bath water. Her voice once again multiplied and harmonized like it had when she healed him as he was resting on his couch in his living room, which now seemed so long ago that it could have happened last year.

Her touch made Curtis feel stronger, better. Then it changed and he felt something he didn't like. The warmness she created in him began to centralize in his back. It started to burn and hurt. As he held onto Charlie with one arm, and tried to pull Vivica with the other, he didn't know what to do about the burning in his back.

"Charlie, what are you doing?" Curtis felt his blood pressure rising and his anger building up. "Charlie you need to help Daddy save Mommy, but what you are doing is hurting me. Charlie that burns! Stop!"

"You need to let it out, Curtis," Charlie said in a deep voice that was not her own. Still, in the background, the soft humming of the four year old continued.

"Let it out," Charlie said, looking at Curtis. The innocent eyes of Curtis's daughter were now replaced with the experienced eyes of a much older soul. "Let it out... NOW!"

Charlie squeezed Curtis's arm. The burning in Curtis's back pierced his skin, tearing it and his shirt open. Two wings, one black and one white, unfolded out of the muscles and the bones of his back. They flared out, stretching high and wide. A magnificent power pulsed through him and an invincible god-like strength consumed him. Curtis screamed out in a combination of extreme pain and exhilaration.

"Now save her," said Charlie's altered voice.

With Curtis's arm still stretched out, he felt his energy envelop Vivica's body entirely. He now held her – alone. Curtis pulled her with all his might and within a few seconds Vivica was standing at his side.

Vivica couldn't comprehend what had just happened. She heard Curtis scream and then watched as two very large, angelic wings forced themselves out of his back. She felt his embrace and then instantly she was standing next to him and Charlie. She was relieved to be away from Eve, but now that she was standing next to Curtis she noticed he had the face of her husband but his body was different. He was taller. Stronger. And, of course, this Curtis had wings.

"Mommy," Charlie said in her young voice and leaped from Curtis's side onto Vivica, barreling her over onto the uneven plateau.

Eve looked over at Curtis, his wings spread wide, and at Vivica and Charlie on the ground.

In the meantime, Adam had crossed the grassy circle towards Joshua's suspended hand and his talisman. He couldn't see beyond the hand; the world outside the iron ring barrier was kept hidden from him, as though he was a fish inside a golden, opaque bowl. It didn't matter to Adam if he could see the earth yet or not because he knew Eve was somewhere close at hand. His beautiful wife, Eve. With all of her past attempts to free him from his prison, he had never been this close to her. He wasn't sure if it was real or imagined, but Adam could smell the faint fragrance of apple blossoms that drifted into the hallowed circle. With the hand of the descendant of David in front of him, Adam reached out and cupped his hand over Joshua's. The stone idol containing Joshua's blood was the coupling instrument that fused the two souls. The link was strong; Joshua was truly an heir of David. Now Adam waited for the sacrifice that would briefly split the barrier between the worlds and allow him back into theirs.

Curtis watched as Adam grabbed Joshua's hand. He bent down and pulled apart the ropes still binding Vivica with his bare hands. His new strength snapped them easily.

"Vivica, run! Get Charlie out of here."

Vivica didn't know what to make of her husband but she understood she had to get Charlie off the plateau. Standing up, she took her daughter into her arms and headed for the idling Range Rover.

"Kill her!" Eve said to Joshua. "She has served her purpose."

Without blinking an eye or shifting his posture, Joshua pulled a small caliber pistol out from his pocket, and within less than a second he fired two rounds into Vivica's back. One of the bullets passed through Vivica's heart, killing her instantly. As her body fell to the ground, she tossed Charlie wide; in her very last act of her life she was still trying to protect her daughter.

"MOMMY!" Charlie screamed as she landed hard and tumbled into the grass.

"Don't worry, Charlie, you will be with her soon," Eve said and raised her hand. Eve's action forced Charlie to her feet and pulled her towards the circle.

Curtis watched Vivica's body fall and instantly felt her leave this world. "NO!" he screamed.

He slowed the world down when he saw Eve reach out for Charlie, but the world wasn't slowing; Charlie was still quickly heading towards Eve. Curtis materialized the black two-headed sword and ran with all of his might to reach Charlie before Eve did. Half way across the plateau, it was apparent to Curtis that he was going to be late. But she was not taking Charlie from him too. With rage and desperation he leaped into the air and raised his sword high above his head ready for the attack. The wind picked Curtis up by his wings, blasting high above the ground. He flew over Joshua's head and landed straight down in front of Eve. Curtis brought his sword down with unbelievable fury. The speed Curtis possessed was supernatural, but Eve watched the Nephilim attack and was unimpressed. Easily anticipating the strike, Eve took a step backwards, leaving Charlie in front of her.

With all of Curtis's gifts and speed he couldn't stop or even slow his sword.

The word "Daddy!" from Charlie's voice hung delicately in the air. Confused, Curtis didn't understand what had just happened. Somehow, Eve now stood two feet back from where he knew her to be; she was safely out of reach of his sword – and smiling. Her eyes danced with delight.

"You did it," she breathed. "The sacrifice has been made."

Sacrifice? Slowly, Curtis's eyes trailed from Eve's smile down to his sword. With the force of his thrust, the sword had sunk deep into the plateau. The point of his sword was not surrounded by grass or rock, but by a small, motionless form dressed in pajamas. A tiny hand still gripped a pink blanket that mercifully covered her face. It took several seconds before Curtis realized what he was looking at. He gently rocked the blade back and forth, freeing it from the ground; blood, grass, and mud clung to its sides.

Curtis let the sword fall from his hand and dropped to his knees. "Charlie! Charlie!" Curtis yelled to the small form as he pulled the blanket off of her face. As he looked at her lifeless form, his soul disintegrated. In less than sixty seconds, everything in the world that meant something to him was taken away. He watched the man, Joshua, shoot and kill Vivica, and now, with his own sword, with his own hands, he had murdered his daughter.

Frantically, Curtis grabbed Charlie and pulled her up into his arms. He pressed her face into his chest, close to his heart. His wings instinctively closed around the two of them.

"AHHHHH!"

"Yes, Curtis, it hurts. But her sacrifice will live on forever. I promise."

Joshua looked at the happy face of Eve and then down at Curtis, screaming, his wings were like a large black and white blanket wrapped around him and his child. An incandescent blue light shot out from between the slits and gaps in Curtis's wings. Joshua felt a coldness enter his hand and make its way up his arm.

Yes I can feel your heart beat. The gateway is opening. Adam's voice spoke clearly in Joshua's head. The sacrifice of the child, the release of her soul, bridged the gateway between the two worlds. Eve walked around Curtis's slumped form and up to Joshua.

"Come to me, my love," she said looking into Joshua's eyes. She placed her hands on each side of his face, behaving as if Adam was already inhabiting Joshua's body.

Adam spoke faintly through Joshua's lips. "I am coming, my wife. I am almost through."

Eve leaned in and kissed Joshua's mouth. Lightning again began to crack and spider throughout the celestial cloud.

Even though Curtis was engulfed in the blue, luminescent glow, his world was black. He kissed the top of Charlie's head. It was still warm and still smelled like his little girl. Then, the sadness ended. As if someone pulled a plug, it was drained out of him, leaving a void within him, a vacuum, a hole.

For Curtis, the world stopped. Then he felt the heat. Rage blasted into him. It not only filled the void, but overflowed it. He was no longer a husband or a father. When Eve took that from him she made him into someone else, something else. He was now an instrument of death.

The familiar voice of Lucifer filtered through the deafening humming in his head. "Curtis, I ordain you the Angel of Vengeance and proclaim your new name throughout the cosmos as Bosszúel. Stand Bosszúel, deliver your revenge."

With the last vestige of his humanity, he gingerly laid Charlie's corpse back down on the grass. With his wings still cupped around him, and his mercury-silver eyes now blinding white, he grabbed the black sword. In a flash, he was standing behind Joshua. He looked at Eve over Joshua's shoulder as she withdrew her lips. Seeing the Nephilim staring at her, Eve took a step back.

"It is happening, Curtis, you can't stop it. Adam is here," Eve said, startled by his appearance, both visually and by the simple fact he was standing in front of her.

"He is not here yet, and my name is Bosszúel," the Angel of Vengeance replied. Inside the golden cloud of the Nether World voices repeated and echoed his name *Bosszúel, Bosszúel*. In the blink of an eye, Bosszúel raised his sword and brought it down over Joshua's forearm, cutting off

Joshua's hand, and severing his connection with Adam and the other realm.

"AHHH!" Dual screams escaped from Joshua's body: one from him and the other from Adam.

"NO!" Eve yelled. At the same time, Joshua grabbed what remained of his arm and pulled it into his chest.

"He isn't fully across," Eve said, "His soul cannot be exposed to this realm." With her left hand, Eve grabbed Joshua by the throat to hold him in place, and with her right hand she grabbed his amputated arm, trying to reconnect the path for Adam's transition.

"ADAM," Eve screamed his name. Joshua squirmed, trying to pull away, but Eve held him easily.

Bosszúel swung his sword up between Joshua's legs and out through the top of his skull, dividing him completely in half. Joshua's body slipped from between Eve's fingers and hit the ground heavy and wet. The cloud inside the circle erupted into a chaotic storm of lightning and fire.

Adam finally released his grip of the talisman, but it was already too late. His soul had breached the boundary of the sanctified ring, and in doing so he violated the *Caelestis Exilium*; he broke the divine law of his imprisonment. Still tethered to Joshua's hand on the inside of the circle, Adam burst into flames. Screaming, he flailed his arms around like a mad man.

"Adam, come to me," Eve yelled to him, but Adam could no longer hear her. Instead, he staggered backwards towards the Jacob's Ladder. His soul burned with the intense fires of the cursed Hell. Demons and lost spirits that were also trapped in the Nether World made their way down the stairway in a free-for-all towards Joshua's palm: the open doorway out of their world and into Bosszúel's. They fought rapaciously to fit themselves through the tiny opening. Like rats scurrying off a sinking ship one at a time, they fit through the open porthole. The lightning barrage inside the ring vapourized any demons and spirits that got caught waiting their turn to escape. Bosszúel did nothing about the cursed individuals that did escape; he did not care. They hurried away from the plateau and out into the Irish country-side repeating his name, *Bosszúel*.

Instead, Bosszúel stared at Eve. The Angel of Vengeance raged inside of him like a rabid dog that had just broken free of his leash.

Eve, on the other hand, stared at her husband who was screaming in pain. Adam stumbled and fell as he tried to make his way back to the ladder and back to the Nether Realm where the fire would be extinguished and his soul could wait for Eve to try again.

He picked himself up and stumbled again. He could feel his divine life force leave him as the fire used it for fuel. Almost blinded by the flames, he crawled his way to the base of the ladder. As he climbed up the first two steps, the occupants of the realm trampled him on their way down.

“Off of me,” Adam screamed at them. “I am the *First One*. I was created in HIS image.”

But the despicable phantoms and specters no longer feared Adam; he had only half of the divinity that he possessed just moments before, and it was rapidly deteriorating.

Eve’s heart broke as she watched her husband being kicked and stepped on like some lesser being: an angel or a human. She stared at him and Bosszúel stared at her.

“The time is not yet right, Bosszúel,” Lucifer whispered again in his head. “They are still linked and she is still very powerful. Give me my moment. Then, you can take yours.” Bosszúel nodded his head. His fingers turned and rolled the sword in his hand.

In a slight ease from the mass exodus of the Nether Realm, Adam stood himself up, shaking and weak.

"Where do you think you are going?" Lucifer asked, standing behind Adam. With his white wings stretched out wide, he wore a red leather Roman chest plate and a gold battle helmet with a red plume. In his right hand he held a flaming staff where his Seraphim sword once was.

Lightning continued to blast the inner circle. Adam turned around, swaying and rocking; he could hardly stand.

"What dost thou want, snake charmer?"

"You are coming with me, Adam. Your divinity is mine; I have need of it," Lucifer said, satisfaction gleamed from his face.

"Thou cannot touch me. I am the First One. I am the *First One*," Adam shouted.

Adam caught a bolt of lightning in his hand and attempted to throw it at Satan, but instead of a deadly blast of electricity, it harmlessly shot wide and fizzled on the ground. Adam was so weak that the movement caused him to slip and fall onto the steps like a drunkard on a roadside curb.

"My, how you have fallen," Lucifer mocked, taking great pleasure in Adam's humiliation. Satan raised his staff and launched it into the Jacob's Ladder, causing it to explode. The fine, dust-like particles of Jennifer Leary showered down and drifted away into the light breeze coming off of the ocean. Adam dropped down into the grass.

"Thou can't take me, Ha-Sata," Adam said, looking up at him from the ground. The lightning from the cloud finally ceased and the fire burning off of Adam was almost out.

"Thou understand Yahweh's law. I am untouchable."

"That was before all of this," Lucifer said, stepping closer and gesturing to the circle. "He's let you go. You are now a *free agent*."

"That is impossible," Adam said, swallowing hard. "Thou is a false prophet; a liar."

Lucifer grinned. "Adam, Adam, Adam. Come to me, old friend. Give me a hug." Satan stretched out his arm and Adam rose to his feet. Without touching the ground, Adam drifted closer.

"Thou dost not discomfort me," Adam said as he looked into Satan's eyes.

"That's because you have never known fear. Let's remedy that, shall we?" Lucifer replied and embraced Adam with both arms.

Thousands of small shadows from the uneven plateau slithered their way over to Satan, forming a dark square beneath his feet. Adam and Lucifer dropped down into it and out of sight.

Eve screamed in horror as she watched them disappear.

"She's all yours," Lucifer's voice whispered into Bosszúel's ear.

Bosszúel shifted the two-headed sword in his fingers one last time, and then plunged the double-headed end into Eve's stomach and up into her chest cavity while she was still looking away. The impalement got her attention.

The tips probed out of her chest, just below her collar bone, causing her Abaya to pop out from her body like two tents. Eve's beautiful face twisted and distorted, more from the agony of losing her husband – maybe once and for all – than from having one meter of celestial blade deep inside of her. She took a step closer into Bosszúel's space. With her left hand she grabbed him by the throat and forced him back three steps. She balled her right hand up tight into a fist and drove it hard into the side of his face. The strike was so powerful that it launched Bosszúel into the air away from the circle. Quickly, her hand shot out, grabbed his foot, and stopped him dead, dropping him to the ground.

Bosszúel lay on the plateau on his back, his wings pressed under him. He looked up, dazed, at the golden cloud; it was dissipating outwards and spreading thin. The gateway was closing.

Still holding Bosszúel by his boot, Eve swung his body up like a rag doll and slammed him down again, this time face first into the ground. Bosszúel couldn't move; the last brutal assault had knocked the air out of his lungs.

"You killed him! You sent him to Hades," Eve shouted, her face still bent and deranged.

Bosszúel didn't move – couldn't move. He just laid face down. Eve dropped his foot and walked up onto his back. She stood there for several seconds and looked down at Bosszúel's motionless body under her feet. Rage built up its pressure inside of her like a volcano just moments before it explodes. Then she erupted. Eve screamed out into the night sky. Weir's Snout shook and rumbled with her ire. The tall towers of stacked basalt blocks along the coastline toppled into the sea and the cliff itself began to give away.

Eve brought down both of her fists onto Bosszúel's back, driving him several more centimeters into the earth. She stepped off to the side of him, looking down in disgust, and then grabbed the base of each wing and hoisted him up over her head. Bosszúel's arms and legs hung limp and defenseless at his sides. Then she threw him into the air. Bosszúel didn't feel himself flying through the air, but he felt the impact of the metal grill, bumper, and hood of the 4x4. Eve stomped her way towards him; she wasn't finished with him yet. The Irish terrain continued to shake as parts of it folded and slid off into the Atlantic, sending plumes of water high into the air behind her.

Bosszúel inhaled weakly. The world around him flashed on and off as he slipped in and out of it. Steam jetting out from the crumpled radiator, combined with offset headlamp beams, added to the scene's eerie and nightmarish atmosphere. With each of Bosszúel's revivals, Eve was a step closer. The handle of the sword still protruded out of her abdomen, affecting her no more than an irritating sliver. And, at the moment, her attention was on something else.

Eve grabbed Bosszúel by the face and pulled him out of the concave indent that his body had created. In an apocalyptic-like event, the ground behind Eve split apart as the remainder of the plateau crumbled and gave way to the ocean. The iron ring of the circle, and the bodies of Joshua, Vivica, and little Charlie went with it. The coastline had been reshaped.

Eve forced Bosszúel to his knees in front of her.

"Your blood line ends here. It ends tonight," she said, looking down at him. "When you get to Hades, tell Ha-Sata I am coming for him next."

There was nothing Bosszúel could do but wait for the end that was sure to come. His eyes fell on the handle of his sword. *Even my sword won't kill her*, he thought to himself. *I don't care. Just end this so I can be with my family.* Then somehow – for some inexplicable reason – Bosszúel – Curtis remembered Lucifer's comments: *"It has never been done. It should never have been done."*

"Then maybe I should undo them," Bosszúel said out loud and grabbed hold of the handle with both hands.

"You're pathetic, Curtis or *whoever* you are now. A sword can't kill me."

"What about two swords?" Bosszúel threw his arms wide, pulling the Cherubim and Seraphim swords apart and separating them once again from each other. Bosszúel held the bone handle of Lucifer's sword in his right hand and white marble handle of Jophiel's in his left. "And the name is *Bosszúel.*"

Eve looked down and watched an arm fall into the grass, followed by lumps of bloody flesh falling at her feet, not yet realizing that they belonged to her.

The swords cut through Eve easily, and now Bosszúel was staring into an open chest crowned with the white ends of Eve's severed rib cage. The workings of a beating heart and expanding lungs moved in front of him while other organs slid out onto the ground.

Eve stood frozen, not knowing what to do. Bosszúel seized the opportunity. He jumped to his feet and with a blade in each hand he swung them in front of him. Jophiel's blade cut through Eve's neck at the same time that Lucifer's blade sliced through her torso. Eve's eyes went wide.

"You may live forever, but you're not doing it up here," Bosszúel said and kicked her off of the cliff and onto the remains of the collapsed plateau. Her body, divided into three, somersaulted out of sight and into the Atlantic Ocean's high tide.

***

48 Hours Later

Curtis sat on his couch, unshaven and unclean. He had spent two days sinking deeper and deeper into depression. Jerry Kraft, John Christmas, and Angus Maclean had all stopped by, and each time Curtis ignored the door. Even Lin from Lin's Wok stopped by with a bowl of soup that she had to leave on the front step. With the curtains and shades drawn tight, their good intentions never cast any positive light into the darkness that had consumed both the interior of Curtis's home and his soul.

Eavery finally walked into the living room. Curtis sat motionless, except for the movement of his index finger that traced the outline of Vivica's face inside the wooden frame. Charlie's first blanket and several of her stuffed teddy bears shared the sofa cushion. The air was thick and stale.

"This place stinks and you look like shit," Eavery scolded. Sphinx circled himself in and out of Eavery's feet, meowing.

"When is the last time you fed your cat?"

"You weren't there," Curtis said, not taking his eyes off Vivica's face. "I needed your help – you're a fucking God! I saved the fucking world but I couldn't even save my family. And I believe I even sold my soul to the God of the Underworld. If I could make that choice again, the world would be a very different place than it is today." Tears streamed down his cheeks. "I needed you… they needed you."

Eavery crossed the room and took the recliner. "I am sorry, Curtis. I am limited with where I can go and what I can do. As a God, I'm pretty dead. But you, Curtis, you are still alive. Don't destroy yourself like this. Let me help you. Let your friends help you."

"Get out of my house. Leave me alone and take the bloody cat with you."

Eavery leaned in closer to his friend. "Curtis… don't end it this way."

"It's Bosszúel, haven't you heard? GET OUT! Before this does end badly," Curtis raised his silver eyes to Eavery.

"All right," Eavery said. He stood up and walked through the front window, but not before throwing open the curtains. The bright, summer sunlight flooded the living room, almost sanitizing the air.

"Son of a bitch!" Curtis yelled out after Eavery. The light burned his eyes that had become accustomed to the dark and gloomy environment. Curtis stood up in haste to once again close out the light, and in doing so he dropped the picture of Vivica onto the floor, breaking the glass pane spotted with mucus, drool, and tears.

"NO!" Curtis cried as he watched the crack split across Vivica's face and heard the crisp snap of the glass. "No, no, no, noooo!" He dropped to his knees and sobbed uncontrollably. Not only couldn't he save his wife, but he couldn't even save a visual representation of her. He felt like he was at the end of what was left of his sanity. Under his breath he cursed himself for dropping the picture.

Then Curtis felt as if someone ran a finger up his spine. The sensation seemed to pull him out of his body. Curtis stared down, watching himself cry. He looked on from the sidelines as the last several seconds rewound themselves. It felt like a kind of twisted, manufactured *remembering*. He could see the pathetic mess that he had become sitting on the sofa; Vivica's picture was back on his lap, and the glass pane was as good as new – albeit grungy. Finally, the timescale reversed itself again and the scene played forward. He observed Eavery throw open the curtains and disappear through the window.

A flash of light, like the brilliant snap of a camera bulb, lit the room. It was quicker than a blink, but inside that moment, as Curtis looked down at himself, he thought he saw another *him* standing off to the right. A third Curtis with a confused expression looked at him standing over himself. Like a phantom blip on a RADAR screen, as fast as he spotted him, he was gone.

"Son of a bitch!" his other self shouted. Reactively, Curtis looked down and reached out to stop himself from dropping the picture – again. The instant he touched his other self, the vision popped, and he was standing in his own body once again, looking out of his own eyes at the undamaged picture. Curtis examined the frame.

"Did I *actually* drop the picture, or did I just hallucinate the whole thing?" he asked out loud. Curtis tenderly put the picture back down on the end table. The sun light reflected off of Vivica's smiling face. It pierced the humid and dusty air like a beacon through a thick fog. And like the maritime icon of days past, it guided Curtis out of the dangerous darkness. Sensing a break in his mindset, Sphinx let out a bellowing meow down at his feet.

"You want some food, don't you pal?"

Curtis refilled Sphinx's dish with a cup of dry kibble and gave him some fresh water. Sphinx purred away contentedly. While the cat gorged himself, Curtis climbed into the shower. The intense heat from the hot water burned his skin red and filled the small bathroom with steam like a sauna. It wasn't until the hot water turned cold that Curtis began to feel clean. As he stepped over the edge of the tub and onto the bath mat, a mark on the window glass caught his attention. The steam brought back the line he drew on the glass a week earlier when he added a mustache to what he incorrectly guessed was Charlie's self-portrait. Curtis reached over with his finger and doodled her face around the line. His finger tip squeaked and squawked on the damp glass. It was a horrible likeness, but for the first time in days Curtis smiled.

He pulled on a pair of loose shorts and a t-shirt and sat down at the dining room table with a large bowl of Mini-Wheats cereal. He lost himself watching Sphinx bat around a small Styrofoam ball Charlie had used as part of her art and craft inventory. Sphinx's paws frantically slipped and slid on the hardwood floor. Curtis spotted a small bale of wheat on the table beside his bowl; it must have fallen out. In his daze, he bent back his forefinger and flicked the cereal.

"Here, play with this," he said to the pet.

Instead of adding another toy to Sphinx's arsenal of distractions, it bounced off the back of his head and sent the little feline running for his life.

"Sorry!" Curtis yelled out, feeling bad for wrecking his fun but giggling all the same.

I wonder if I could take it back, he thought to himself.

Exhaling, Curtis tried to lull himself back into the zone he felt earlier with Vivica's broken picture – but without the desperation and emotional breakdown.

Curtis tried to focus and channel all of his concentration and all of his divine energy on replaying the events that led up to the cat being assaulted by high fibre. If he allowed himself, Curtis would have laughed at that thought.

Then, like earlier, Curtis felt the finger stroke up his spine. And before he could think about it, he was standing beside himself again. He watched a very comical scene: Sphinx was slipping and skidding backwards towards the location of the "incident." He watched the tiny square of cereal fly back up onto the table and under his finger. Curtis stared at himself in disbelief.

What the hell have I become? What kind of creature can manipulate time at will? Who am I? What am I? When this first happened at the sofa, Curtis thought it was more likely that he was having a mental breakdown than that he could manipulate time. It was easy to convince himself that he never did break the glass pane inside of the picture frame. He believed that dividing himself into two separate Curtises was a vivid hallucination caused by the lack of food and sleep for days, combined with the devastation of losing his family, and giving up his soul.

Curtis stepped sideways and examined himself sitting at the table. A freeze framed, three-dimensional, high definition image of himself was sitting there with a smirk on his face. Curtis crouched down in front of himself in the direct flight path of the cereal. He stared into his own eyes; he saw creases from age reaching out of the corners (something he had never paid much attention to before). He examined his own face the way others might see him. The sparse strands of silver that blended into his bangs. The pain.

No, Curtis wasn't staring at a holographic picture of himself. No, the Curtis in front of him was very real.

Curtis touched the shoulder of his freeze-framed self, sending himself back into his own body. He looked at the cereal and picked it up.

"I can do it!" he yelled out ecstatically. This time he picked up the dry square and dropped it into his bowl.

CHAPTER THIRTY-SEVEN

Maria Elena, Chile

The brakes to the rusted out van screeched to a halt at the side entrance of the old monastery. Lenci Balog, a sandy haired man in his fifties and Testvériség veteran, climbed out of the front passenger seat. He put his hands on his hips and stretched out his back.

"Ohhh!" he groaned and repositioned a new red and black Knights of Columbus ball cap on his head.

"Muchas gracias señor," Lenci said, and then handed the driver a 5000 pesos bill.

"Gracias!" the driver returned, smiling.

Lenci turned back to face the inside the van. "Kezdjük munka (*lets get started*)."

The side door squeaked and whined open and thudded hard against the rubber stopper. Lukács and four other men stepped out of the dusty van; each one fitted their ball caps on their heads.

The rough, sand-blasted door to the monastery creaked loudly on its worn hinges. A pudgy, short, balding man wearing an archetypical brown friar's smock poked his head out of the gap; he had a broad grin on his face as he welcomed the strangers. Padre Dominico La Suenza was born in Maria Elena sixty-three years ago tonight, and was currently the only Catholic priest in town. Until now, he was celebrating his birthday by himself.

Lenci spotted the cheerful man and walked over with his hand extended to introduce himself. "Father La Suenza?" he said in a fake American accent. The padre scurried over, his legs rapidly shuffling under his robe.

"Pleez - pleez, Dominico, por favor," he said excitedly, taking Lenci's hand within his two hands, happy to have company on his birthday.

"I am John," Lenci lied, shaking the friar's hand.

"Very good. How was your journey? New York City is quite far from here?"

"It was long, but after a shower and a good night's sleep, we will be ready to get to work first thing in the morning."

"Si. I must admit: I'm surprised you have come. You are aware that there were no survivors to help? The entire Gomez family perished in the fire, God rest their souls," the padre said making the sign of the cross on himself.

"Oh Padre, if there is one thing I have learned, it is that there is always more work to do," Lenci said and gave him a wink.

"Very good. Since the devastating earthquake in '09 there is lots to do around here. Once you and the other Knights have unloaded the van, I can show you to your rooms. I hope you and your men won't mind sharing rooms; it is not a large monastery. Not a great need for a large church any more – not out here, anyway. But the rooms are always clean – always ready."

"That will be much appreciated," Lenci said, and then turned to the van. The men pulled out their suitcases and several large black plastic Pelican cases.

"Luke, Father La Suenza ..." Lenci was interrupted by the priest clearing his throat, "sorry – Dominico – will show us to our rooms. Have the men collect the luggage and follow us up."

Lukács looked over and nodded. Lenci may be the one with the flawless English, but like fuck he was going to take orders from him for the next few days. "O-kay," was Lukács' broken reply.

Lenci clenched his jaw and tried to mask his scolding look from the padre's eyes. As the men entered the eighty year old priory, Lorand Kelemen, or "Paul," glanced over at a vigil of candles burning in front of a six-foot-tall statue of a woman dressed in a brown scapular. Padre La Suenza noticed the man's eyes.

"Ah, Si! She is Maria of Mount Carmel, the matron of our pueblo. Many of the locals will come in and light the candles in her name. You do not recognize the Virgin Mother?"

"She looks different in the brown dress," Lenci jumped in as he looked around deeper into the congressional seating area and along the pews. Lukács looked closer at the base of the statue. It sat on a 5 cm plaster platform that appeared to have etched symbols similar to the ones on the burnt piece of paper Gergõ had shown them. But here on the statue there were dozens. Lenci leaned in closer too.

"Dominico, what are these?" he asked, pointing to the lettering.

"I do not know," the padre replied, brushing it off. "The statue is very old, before my time."

"Huh," Lenci murmured and glanced at Lukács.

Padre La Suenza took them down a sparsely decorated corridor; the wooden floor creaked under the combined weight of the men and their luggage. The corridor ended at an original wooden door and latch dating back to the construction of the monastery. An exposed light bulb mounted into the clay wall was the only source of light within the dim hallway, except for the lit candles at the entrance that created more shadows than they eliminated. When the priest opened the door, the men were flooded with light from the connecting room. Lukács almost shielded his eyes from the glare, but with the added light he could make out more of the ancient script etched around the top of the door frame into the wall. He elbowed Lenci and directed him with his eyes to look up. Lenci nodded back in acknowledgement – *I see it*.

The adjoining room was more like a lobby or foyer. The common room had 5 more wooden doors, four on the men's right side and one on their left. There was also a lone, dirty window straight ahead of them, and several old wooden chairs and tables skirted the walls. The chairs looked weathered and rickety: unsafe. Each table, four in all, held a lit electric lamp, except for one that held a bouquet of dusty, dried-out flowers. The dried flowers were placed between the door on the left and an alcove set into the wall that contained another six-foot-tall statue, this time of a man clutching scrolls in his left hand while his right hand was up blessing anyone that might be walking by. This statue also stood on a raised platform with similar markings.

"These three doors here are your rooms. Unfortunately you will have to share them, but there are two bunks in each. The rooms are quite small so you will probably have to leave your baggage out here. I will lock the doors; they will be safe."

"Where do they lead to?" Lenci asked, pointing to the two remaining doors.

"The fourth door is my room and the last door opposite the others leads into the kitchen. There isn't much food – I live alone – but if you are hungry I have some leftover beans and rice I can heat up rápido," the padre said, smiling.

Lenci eyed the statue and the platform. "Who is this?"

"Why, that is Saint Lawrence, the patron saint of miners." Dominico answered Lenci with a smile, but his mind was questioning why Catholic men of the Knights of Columbus did not recognize pillars of the Church.

Lukács looked around the austere room, examining its interior. He was beginning to feel uncomfortable with the idea of spending the night (or two) in a building specifically built for the religion of the Romans. The look on the other men's faces said they felt the same way. Lenci stepped closer to the statue and traced his finger along the carved script.

"There is a lot of this... writing... around your church. I see you even have it over each of these doors in here," he said as he squared himself off with the elderly priest. "See?"

He pointed his finger around the room. "Is it some kind of prayer or blessing?"

Father La Suenza began to feel and look very uncomfortable. "Like I mentioned earlier: before my time. You gentlemen would probably like to settle down for the night; you must be very tired from your long journey. I too had a long day so if you don't mind..."

"The Gomez's also had this type of script in their home before... the fire," Lenci said and stepped into the padre's personal space. "Are there any more of these families in this shit town?"

Father La Suenza's face hardened by the abrupt change of tone. "I wouldn't know. You're not with the Knights of Columbus, are you? Who are you men – really?"

Lukács turned to the four men. "Csomagolja ki a készüléket (*Unpack the equipment*)."

The men started unlocking and popping open the latches of the Pelican cases. The first case held a large quantity of C4 explosives and detonators. Another case contained five British L85A2 assault rifles with German made 40 mm grenade launchers attached to their undersides and thousands of rounds of ammunition.

Lenci advanced on the priest, grabbed him by the front of his robe and slammed him hard against the wall, knocking over the small table and dried flowers. The glass vase shattered at their feet. Dominico La Suenza stared wide into Lenci's eyes; his body quivered with adrenaline and fear at the attack.

"We too are priests. Brothers of the Testvériség," Lenci said, breathing down on him.

"I know of you," Dominico said. He tried to stand taller, more defiant, but the words shook in his voice and betrayed him. "You want to prevent mankind from ever learning of God's words."

"The Knowledge is not meant for mankind, priest," Lukács barked from around Lenci's shoulder.

"Luke, attend to the equipment," Lenci ordered, his eyes and grasp never moved from the old man.

Lukács stared at the back of Lenci's head; he burned from the insult of being talked down to, especially from Lenci Balog, a man whose station was equal to his own within the Testvériség, and who decided on his own to lead the operation so he could better his position. "Paul" reached over and passed Lukács a tactical assault pistol and a clip from a third case. Lukács slapped in the clip and inserted the weapon into a hidden pocket inside of his jacket.

"Now Padre – excuse me – Dominico, where are the scripts you have been working on and who else has been helping you? Tell me the names and addresses and we will only hit those heretics. Otherwise, we will kill everyone in this town – just to be on the safe side. And, believe me," Lenci smiled, "we can."

Father La Suenza looked down at the cache of explosives as one of the men pushed the case aside.

"Then you will have to. God has already prepared my soul."

"James, Mark, megragad egy kar (*grab an arm*)," Lenci called over his shoulder, keeping protocol by still using their code names. The two men put down the rifles they were loading. "Mark" grabbed the padre's right arm and pinned it to the wall as "James" did the same to the left. Lenci let go the old man's robe and took a few steps back, looking him over.

"You know, Dominico, Luke here is a fantastic marksman. He has killed people from over a kilometer away; they never even knew he was there. But me, I like to see their eyes."

Lenci fished in his pocket and pulled out an 8 cm long charcoal grey blade. He expertly let it tumble and twirl around his fingers as he played with it. He squeezed the blade with his fingers and the one knife divided into two equally long but thinner knives. The three men watched Lenci show off his talent like some kind of street performer. Lukács exhaled loudly, hoping Lenci would get the hint and carry on with the interrogation. This was going to take all night as it was; he didn't need to sit there and watch Lenci's show.

If Lenci heard Lukács' exasperated attempt to rush him, he didn't show it. Instead, he carried on his act by pretending to almost drop the blade but then magically recover it at the last second.

Lukács rolled his eyes. "Gyerünk (*come on*)."

With a bullet fast snap of his elbow, Lenci sent a blade into the padre's right wrist. The knife sunk deep into the clay wall. Another quick snap and the second blade pinned the padre's left wrist to the wall.

"Ahhh," Dominico screamed. Pain shot through the priest's arms as the knives secured them in place so that he was unable to move. The two men stepped away and continued unloading the cases and prepping the weapons.

"Now, you look like a Christian," Lenci remarked over Father La Suenza's screams and mockingly held out his arms and tilted his head to the side. "Give me the names, or I will kill every man, woman, and child in this fucking town."

The padre looked over at his right wrist and watched his blood make its way down the wall. Then he looked at the statue of St. Lawrence. Under his breath, he mumbled some prayers in Spanish, and then the old priest started to shake as he went into shock.

"He's not going to tell us. I think he needs some more persuasion," Lukács said to Lenci.

"When you're right, Luke, you are right. Start placing the explosives, and make sure you get that fire truck."

Lenci bent over and dug deep into his luggage bag, and pulled out a large 34 cm hunting knife inside a black Kevlar carrying sheath. He slid the blade out and stepped closer to the padre. He marveled at the blade with the awe-like fascination that only the truly psychotic would possess.

"Last chance, Padre, to make amends for your grievous sins. Last chance to save any innocent lives in this town... if there are any. Confession is more your deal than ours, but I am willing to listen."

Drool hung long off Dominico La Suenza's lip. His breathing came in short gasps as waves of pain traveled up from his wrist and into his chest. "The *Knowledge* from heaven was given to man... from the angels of God. It is our birth right. When we... share that knowledge, then all of mankind will truly be free."

Lenci Balog had heard enough. Without any more hesitation, he pushed the 34 cm blade straight into the priest's chest, dividing his rapidly beating heart into two, killing him instantly. When he arrived at the monastery, he knew instinctively that he was going to have to kill the old priest, but he thought he was going to have more fun with him first. He thought maybe he'd hang the priest from his arms and slice his stomach open, spilling his internal organs onto the floor in front of him – like they did in the good ole' days – but today he guessed he just wasn't up for it. He noticed as he got older that he didn't enjoy the killing as much anymore; it was still necessary and he still did it, but his heart just wasn't *into* it like it once was. Oh well, the priest was still dead, and with him much of the Knowledge.

"You didn't give him much time to talk," Lukács said, now anticipating a lot more work.

"He wasn't going to tell us anything anyway," Lenci defended as he pulled his knife out of the padre's chest and cleaned it on his robe. "And whatever we did force out of him would have been a lie."

Paul paused, pocketing clips of ammunition, and looked up at the writing on the walls. "I wouldn't have guessed the monastery was involved, but I suppose it makes sense," he said in full Hungarian.

James packed another cube of C4 into a shoulder bag. "Where do you suppose he learned it?"

"I don't know," Mark added, also returning to his native language. He walked over to the statue of St. Lawrence, "But it's even on their statues. It must go way back."

They watched Mark as he cocked his shoulder back and struck the sculpture with the butt of his rifle. Instead of shattering, the figure gave a hollow *"pock"* sound and partially crumbled in on itself. The five men looked at each other and then at St. Lawrence. Lukács stepped up to the tall ceramic figure, grabbed it by the scrolls in the statue's hand, and pulled the figure forwards, toppling it over onto its face. The hollow ceramic effigy cracked further. On the back of the statue were two raised nubs; something had been removed and sanded down a long time ago.

"I think this statue had wings once," Paul said as the men gathered around.

"I think it used to be a statue of an angel," Mark added.

Lenci knelt down and examined the figure. Then he struck one of the cracks that had formed from the fall with the base of his knife, spreading it further. It took several more strikes before the relic split apart, not exposing an empty center as they expected, but revealing that it concealed something. Lenci and Paul pulled the old and brittle statue apart like hyenas ravaging the carcass of a fresh kill. Inside the hollow there appeared to be what looked like three large scrolls. The men stared at the open back of the statue and at its contents, astounded by the unexpected find. The room quickly filled with a combination of the stale air from inside of the statue, the ancient musk coming off of the primeval scrolls, and the copper/tin odour of the fresh blood that was still oozing out of the dead priest.

Lenci gently pulled out a scroll, careful not to damage it on any of its jagged ends. It was heavier than it looked and much thicker than modern parchment. To Lenci's fingers it felt like vellum: calf hide. Slowly he unrolled it. Like an old man stretching out his bones first thing in the morning, the parchment opened with a hundred snaps and cracks. The men's eyes widened as the angelic Nephilim script – written on the scroll 5000 years – earlier, was not only legible, but also looked as though it had been written with a deep, metallic-green ink just yesterday. Upon looking at the holy writing, the Testvériség priests quickly began reciting the Ascension Prayer – all except for Lenci. During the prayer, Lukács watched Lenci gently roll the scroll back up and place it on the top of a closed Pelican case. Then he pulled out his satellite phone.

"Yes, this is Balog... No, better than we expected. So far three of the original scrolls... Yes... Yes... I understand."

When Lenci was done with the phone, he put it back into his pocket and emptied out the duffle bag that contained James's clothes. Gently, he inserted the scroll into it, stretching the bag to make it fit.

"What are you doing?" Lukács demanded. The men turned and looked at Lenci.

"New orders," Lenci returned. "Paul, collect those two other scrolls and come with me," he said, still keeping with the code names. "We need to search the other statues and find whatever scrolls are here. Luke, take the other men and carry on with the elimination of the town."

Lukács grabbed Paul's wrist before he could reach for the scroll still inside the statue's cavity.

"You're not taking those scrolls anywhere. Our orders – from the Vezető, are to wipe out every bit of evidence of the script. That script," Lukács fired back, pointing to the scroll Lenci had just placed inside the duffle bag.

"The Társadalom is about to go under new management. Mátyás will no longer be the Vezető."

Lukács looked at Lenci like he had gone mad.

"He was when we left Veszprém yesterday. John, you're about to commit mutiny."

"It is more of a coup, a kind of KRÁJCÁR Spring," Lenci corrected.

"It's still punishable by death. James, Mark, take *Lenci Balog* and secure him until I can talk with the Vezető. Shoot him if he tries to stop you," Lukács ordered.

Lenci smiled to himself at hearing his true name said aloud. It was a purposeful break in protocol that Lukács meant as an insult – after all, the chance of any electronic devices capturing their conversation here in the monastery was extremely low.

The two men looked at each other uncomfortably. The unit rapidly deteriorated as each man tried to judge who was right and who was wrong. Deciding Lukács was more in command, Mark and James stepped towards Lenci, reaching for their weapons, but two slugs quietly *popped* from Paul's pistol. Both Mark and James dropped down dead in mid stride from a bullet hole between the eyes.

Lukács looked down at the gun in Paul's hand; the suppressor attached to the end of the pistol was smoking. Lukács had witnessed the end of many men – shit, he was often the cause of it – and he knew eventually that he would meet his own. It looked as though now he was finally going to be sent into the afterlife to ride horseback on the great

Hungarian Plains with the Prophet Attila; he just didn't expect the end would come from one of his own.

"Sorry, Luke, I know how fond you are of Gergõ, but the KRÁJCÁR is headed in a new direction. No longer are we crusaders to an old religion. This script will ensure a new Testvériség, a new KRÁJCÁR, a new world order. Too bad you won't be around to see it."

Lukács stared at Lenci, took to his knees and bowed his head. He closed his eyes and whispered the KRÁJCÁR prayer, "Words of Strength." Paul looked over at Lenci, uncertain of what to do. Lenci nodded for Paul to shoot Lukács. That moment was all Lukács needed to unload a 15-round clip from his assault pistol into Paul. In a split second, Lenci dove through the door that Father La Suenza said led to the kitchen. Paul crumpled to the floor as bullets struck him in the chest, throat and head. Lukács quickly grabbed the pistol out of Mark's dead grip and sent two rounds into the door frame after Lenci. Ready to spring forward like a sprinter, Lukács reached his left hand out to the fallen and broken statue to steady himself. He was scarcely aware of the jagged edges of the statue's open back but when he touched the cool surface of the ancient manuscript, it pulled his concentration.

Lukács felt his blood drain from him. It left him cold and disoriented, a sensation he had never before experienced. His first instinct was that he had been shot, but surely the impact from the round would have knocked his balance off kilter or even killed him. Perhaps Lenci had another blade hidden up his sleeve and he landed one somewhere in him, and the adrenaline was preventing his body from feeling the pain – a surprisingly common occurrence in his line of work.

As Lukács' mind tried to rationalize what was happening to him, everything within the room stopped. Drops of blood released from Father La Suenza's impaled wrists were somehow floating in mid-air, defying gravity. Splinters of wood that had exploded out from the door frame as a result of the violent impact of the pistol rounds were also ignoring the laws of physics as the tiny shards halted from their natural trajectory and suspended themselves mid-flight.

Lukács looked around the room at the unnatural stillness – the supernatural stillness. His senses (including the common one) screamed that something was wrong. He could no longer smell the Chilean dust that coated just about everything, or the ancient, musky vellum scrolls. Absent were the smells of burnt gunpowder and death that saturated the room only seconds ago. It was as if the Prophet Attila himself was watching Lukács' life and he hit the pause button in the middle of the action scene to go and get some more popcorn. Except in this frozen frame Lukács was still able to move.

No matter what his senses were telling him, Lukács knew Lenci had darted through that doorway and Lukács was going after him. Lukács stood up to step over the statue, but when he did the room pixilated and dissolved away. The brightly-lit monastery was replaced by a moonlit night. He found himself standing outside near an enormous well: a pool of water encased in plaster and stone. A beautiful woman, resting on the edge of the well, sat crying into her hands. She wore an embroidered linen robe dyed red, purple, black, and fuchsia with a head and shoulder scarf that matched. He could hear sounds of a battle taking place in the distance. He heard screams and yells, and the tinning clang of swords. The glow from a large fire lit the horizon somewhere beyond the trees.

"Over here!" a man's voice said from somewhere deep in the darkness.

"Dost thou see him? Is it thy son, Haduj?" the woman cried out, standing up and stepping towards the voice. The man brought a boy barely in his teen years huffing and puffing to the woman. She grabbed the boy tight, almost squeezing the remaining breath out of him.

"Give praise to Arba, thy son returns," she prayed, kissing the top of his head.

For the first time, Lukács noticed he was looking upward at the three strangers; even the teenager towered over him. They were all dressed in some kind of ancient garments – something like what was worn by the Canaanites – only wealthier, perhaps more Egyptian. Lukács didn't know; his fashion history references didn't go much beyond the 1960s, but the clothing looked biblical and luxurious.

The boy carried an open sack slung across his back; it was filled with scrolls similar to the ones found inside the statue.

"Mother, we barely escaped. Men are everywhere... where is father?" Haduj asked, looking up at her.

"He will not... he has been..." she broke down into sobs as she saw visions of her husband's head hanging from the hands of one of the men who sacked their palace. Haduj, a young man in his own right, held his mother up, holding back his own grief.

Another man, the same size of Lukács, caught up to the group with his wife and son. "By the grace of Uriel, thou art secure. My Queen, thou hast made it out of the bloodshed alive, by the grace of Uriel," he said excitedly, very pleased to see his former masters alive.

"Rabdebar? Why dost thou follow? Thy safety and the safety of thy family is thy concern now. We will only attract those murderous men," the woman said as she knelt down to be at the same level as the man.

"Thy husband, Madame, my master, has freed us from thy service, but now more than ever thou dost need Rabdebar," Rabdebar said, holding her large hand in both of his.

"Thou art a free man, Rabdebar, please call me Lilith," she squeezed his hands affectionately and smiled back.

The man that had accompanied Haduj, Ahiman, looked at the group, "We need to reach the Egyptian island colonies in the Hinder Sea. The

Pharaohs have always been good to thy people and are far from the reach of Moses and his men.

Lukács watched the scene play out in front of him. He too became lost in their anxiety and the panic of the moment. There was something about the giant woman that drew him into their life; it was a connection he knew was absurd to even attempt to rationalize, but a familiarity that itched at him all the same. The scene fast forwarded itself as Lukács stood on the sidelines. Days and then weeks of travel by foot passed in just seconds. Although it only took seconds for Lukács to watch their struggles, he got to know them, and feel for them. He shared in their experiences, heard their stories around the night fire, and even cried with them at all they had lost. Their sorrow triggered the grief he had buried decades ago for his tortured and beloved Anya, the mother who loved him too much.

Finally, the small man, Rabdebar, returned one day from the harbour's edge a few gold coins lighter. "We have passage," he said. "Lantis will be thy new home, a safe and prosperous isle firmly in the grasp of the pharaohs."

Lilith hugged her son, and Haduj returned the squeeze. "Our journey is almost over, mother. We can start a new life and leave this nightmare behind us."

Lukács felt relieved for his new family. Lilith allowed a little bit of joy to squeak past the gloom and despair that had consumer her for weeks. Her eyes drifted to Lukács. He knew she couldn't see him – they have never acknowledged his presence – but yet she held his gaze.

"It is almost over, Lilith," Ahiman said, reaching for the hand of his brother's widow.

Lilith continued to stare in Lukács direction. "For some of us, it is only the beginning," she said.

The bustling harbour full of merchants and sailors stopped. The scene before Lukács, frozen in time, pixilated and dissolved around the family of refugees that he had become familiar with and got to know. As the monastery reclaimed his surroundings, Lilith's gaze was the last image to leave him, and for a split second her eyes seemed to float almost magically into the present, not willing to relinquish their connection to Lukács without a fight.

Lukács blinked at the room, momentarily confused. Then life snapped back with ferocity. The shards of wood from the door frame continued their blast outward. What took 1/100th of a second felt like weeks to Lukács. The acidic smell from the burnt gunpowder and the earthly, metallic odour from the blending of dust and blood assaulted his nose. He became nauseous at the heightened atmosphere. Lukács' head swam and he felt as though he was about to pass out, but instead he lurched forward and vomited onto the floor.

Suddenly remembering he was shooting at Lenci, Lukács quickly stood up and ran to the door. On the far side of the kitchen a second door slammed shut.

Lukács leaned against the wall, drained from his vision and his dinner's unexpected return. Looking back at the dead men and the broken statue, he wasn't sure what he should do next. Lenci was gone and Lukács didn't possess the energy to go chase him. And since all of their weapons cache and explosives were here in the room with him, he was quite certain Lenci wouldn't be coming back. Lukács walked back and knelt down beside the statue. He closed his eyes and said a quick prayer for his fallen comrades – but not for the traitor "Paul."

Lukács stared at the two remaining scrolls. "What to do, what to do?" he whispered to himself.

He reached back and grabbed the duffle bag that held one of the scrolls. Gently, he removed the other two scrolls from the effigy and added them to the bag. Zipping it closed, he then grabbed a fresh clip for his gun. Lukács searched the dead padre's pockets and found what he needed: the keys to a ride out of what was soon to become a crater. He then slammed a handful of detonators into a brick of C4, set the remote receiver, and pocketed the transmitter. He closed and locked the Pelican case, grabbed his luggage and duffle bag, and walked out the side door – the same one he entered approximately 60 minutes ago, before his team and his world turned to shit.

Driving out of town in the padre's beat-up Suzuki Vitara, Lukács pressed the buttons on the AM radio until he found a station playing a traditional Salsa beat. As he settled into the dusty seats, he flipped up the safety cover on the transmitter, and, with little afterthought, pulled the lone trigger that vapourized the monastery, the dead priests, and many of the surrounding buildings.

***

Testvériség Debriefing Room 2
Bishop's Palace, Veszprém

"Lukács, I'm very happy to see you have safely returned to us," Elek Szalai said, stepping through the doorway.

"Elek!" Lukács said, surprised to see him and not Gergõ. "I was expecting the Vezető."

Lukács' foot unconsciously brushed up along the black duffle bag, ensuring it was still at his side. Elek's eyes followed the movement.

"He will be here shortly. We received your brief. Are those the scrolls?" His eyes beamed.

"You mean the ones you wanted Lenci to bring back to you – at any cost? *Igen*, these are them."

Lukács stood up and walked around the table, anger welling up inside of him. He wanted to kill the treasonous bastard right there in the debriefing room. If he did, even though Elek deserved it, he would be disgraced and outlawed within the KRÁJCÁR. They would charge *him* for high treason, a crime with only one punishment: death. If he ran (which he would never do), they would commit all their substantial resources on him and hunt him down. It wouldn't take long. Elek wasn't just part of the Társadalom, he was also one of the Group of Seven. He was, for all intentions, untouchable – at least until the trial.

"My heart rejoices that you are still alive. I raised you like a son; I consider you my son," Elek said and gripped Lukács' shoulders in each hand.

"You lying piece of shit." Lukács shrugged off Elek's touch and swallowed hard as he stood his ground. "You have no soul. You want the scrolls, the Knowledge, and the Társadalom. You are not worthy of being Vezető. After your trial when you are tried for treason, I pray to the Prophet that I am the man who gets to pull the trigger." His words stung deep and the pain was evident in Elek's eyes, which brought a little satisfaction to Lukács.

"There is something you need to know about your precious Vezető, Lukács. He is not the loving saviour you think him to be. Grab your bag and come with me." Before giving Lukács a chance to comment, Elek turned and walked out of the room.

Lukács passed through the medieval architecture as he walked down the Grand Hallway of the Bishop's Palace. Suits of armour stood sentinel down each side, always ready. On the walls there were large oil paintings of Attila. Some of the paints showed Attila in battle, sitting on his horse with the Sword of God raised high in the air. Others had Attila riding though a crowd of his men in the glory after the battle. There were twenty-six paintings in total, and in all of them he held the sword.

Elek stopped at a large, heavily-polished oak door on his right; his foot falls still echoing off the stone walls and stairways for several seconds after his last step. He entered the Előkelő Chambers, the meeting room with the English oak table and KRÁJCÁR shield. Lukács halted at the doorway. In his entire life, he had never crossed the threshold. He had never been invited into the noble quarters; it was strictly out of bounds for the Testvériség priests. This was only his second time ever peering into the hallowed room.

Elek noticed he was alone and looked back. Lukács stood at the door. He looked like a child not wanting to enter the Principal's office.

"Come in Lukács, you are my guest." Elek waved his hand, beckoning Lukács forward.

Lukács stared down at the black and gold-checkered carpet inside the room. His foot was heavy and didn't want to move. Normally, such an invitation would be the highlight of his career, but not like this, not today. The honour should be coming from Gergõ Mátyás, the Vezető, the leader of the KRÁJCÁR, and not from this treacherous scum. The gesture made him feel guilty, knowing that his first time in this room would be a dirty secret rather than an admirable and righteous honour.

"Lukács, son, come in and close the door – please."

Hearing this man call him *son* stoked Lukács' rage further, giving his feet something new to think about. Lukács stepped in and closed the giant door. Surprisingly, it shut quietly; the latch from the handle only whispered the click.

"It is time, Lukács, for you to learn the truth about your past."

Lukács walked over and placed the duffle bag down on the floor behind the legs of one of the chairs. At the same time, Elek moved over to the bar and poured two glasses of a decadent Scotch whiskey. Returning, he extended a glass to Lukács.

"Whose truth?" Lukács demanded, staring deep into Elek's eyes and ignoring his offer.

A defeated smile withered on Elek's face as he exhaled through his nose. He placed the glass down on the table.

"Haven't you ever wondered where your father went? Why one day, 39 years ago, he just didn't come home? Haven't you ever wondered what happened to your mother? Lukács, you came to live with me when you were fifteen. You never once asked me where they were."

That was true. Lukács never asked anybody anything; he simply accepted it. He never knew his father and had no memory of him – he died before Lukács could even walk. He was a priest of the Testvériség and Lukács just took it for granted that he was killed during an assignment; it was, after all, a dangerous world. And, as for his disturbed but saintly Anya, he wished to believe that she was happily getting along in a mental institution somewhere. But now, Elek's questioning had planted a seed of doubt in his self deception.

What was Elek's plan? Why this today? It was obvious that Elek was trying to distract him from briefing Gergõ, but did he actually think these games were going to work? But the seed was taking root inside of him. Lukács' eyes fell from Elek. The fires of rage inside of him were doused (just a little) by new suspicions.

Elek continued, "Long before you were born, when your father was still courting your mother, they made a good couple together. They were fun to be around," he said, thinking back to better times.

Lukács watched Elek's face soften at the fond memories.

"Your father, Armand, was quite the joker. You would have liked him."

Amidst everything that was going on, Lukács couldn't believe Elek's audacity to stand there and chat about how cool and fun his father was – a man Lukács never knew. Lukács wanted to reach over and punch him in his face, but at the same time, with equal passion, he yearned to hear more, to learn something about a stranger he spent his life trying not to think about.

“So, one day, he brought your mother in here. He snuck her into this very room, trying to impress her with his ‘connections.’” Elek walked around the room, looking around as the young couple may have done, the way Lukács would have done if he wasn’t focused on controlling his temper. Elek walked over to the glass case that contained the Szentirás Magyar Bible and the three angelic letters. Lukács didn’t even notice the large case was there when he walked in. It was placed against the back wall and impossible to miss – once you’ve seen it and only after you’ve taken in the room’s history and grandeur.

With his back still to Lukács, Elek said, “They came over here and he showed her the Bible. I don’t know if he removed it from the case – he never said – but he showed her the sword.”

CHAPTER THIRTY-EIGHT

"Sword?" Lukács wondered if he hear Elek correctly.

"Yes," Elek said. He turned around and took a sip of the Glenfiddich, pretending to dismiss the relevance of what he had said.

"The Sword of God? The Prophet Attila's holy rapier?" Lukács couldn't believe his ears. *Elek is lying*, Lukács thought, *he must be*.

"Yes."

"You are a liar. That sword was lost – buried with Attila," Lukács raised his voice, offended at being thought a fool.

"No, the sword is here."

"Here in Veszprém?"

"Here," Elek returned.

Lukács did a quick scan of the room. "Here in Bishop's Palace?" His heart was beating heavily and his mind was racing to catch up with it.

"Here, in this very room son. Would you like to see it… the Sword of God?" Elek taunted and sipped the remainder of the golden liquid his glass.

Lukács grabbed the glass of whiskey on the table in front of him and downed it in one swallow. It burned his throat and sinuses as the fumes of the Glenfiddich floated around his nose.

Elek walked over to the wood-paneled wall and tapped his fingers on an unassuming spot. A small hidden door the size of a piece of bread swung open. A digital key pad with randomly sequenced numbers lit the small compartment. Lukács heard a beep acknowledging the correct code. Elek closed the small door. A loud '*pop*' and '*thump*' came from inside the wall and a three-meter by three-meter section of stone wall with the KRÁJCÁR shield mounted to it shifted forward and slid to the left away from Elek, revealing a hidden partition. Inside was the Sword of God just sitting there completely exposed and vulnerable (once the one tonne stone wall was slid to the side). Three spotlights shone down on it – one from the top and the others from opposite sides – illuminating its beauty. Lukács was stunned by its majesty. It hummed as if it drew power from its own glory.

The sword was more than a meter long (closer to four feet) from tip to hilt; it was thin and curved up like a Turkish scimitar. The lights brilliantly reflected off of its golden body. Even though it was exposed to the open air, it was utterly dust free. It looked meticulously polished and cared for. The sword rested on the palms of two solid, golden hands that were mounted at the wrists into the stone wall. The hands held the scimitar as if offering it out to whoever wished to have it. Awestruck, Lukács numbly walked over and stood in front of it.

"It's beautiful, isn't it?" Elek said. His words sounded flat compared to the vibrancy of the sword.

Lettering similar to the Chilean scrolls was etched into the blade: *From One Comes Many.*

Did I read that? Lukács asked himself, and then he reread it again. *That's impossible!*

Lukács couldn't take his eyes off of it. Lukács had tunnel vision: the gleaming sword became the only thing in the room. Finally, with his years of training and discipline, he pulled his eyes away and turned to Elek.

"Why did you show me this? What does this have to do with my Anya and father?"

Lukács eyes wanted to turn back – begged to turn back and look again at the sword – but he forced his head straight. Half of his attention was waiting for Elek's explanation, while the other half focused on keeping his body centered and away from the enchanted rapier.

"Your Anya touched the Isten Kardja," Elek answered.

The mention of the sword's full name beckoned Lukács' eyes back to it.

"I remember your father telling me she seemed to go into a trance, maybe only for a second, but after that touch she was never the same."

Lukács gave in and peered at the sword again; his eyes reread the inscription.

Elek continued, "It started off with nightmares; she would wake screaming in some Semitic dialect. Then she was inflicted with hallucinations. That's when they discovered she was pregnant with you."

My poor, tortured Anya. Thinking back, Lukács always knew she was hiding from something. Grief for his mother's pain filled his heart. Elek left him and returned to the bar to refill the two glasses. Lukács slowly followed him.

"Was she not given medication? Or made to see a psychiatrist?" Lukács asked with a heavy heart.

"We didn't turn to those things back then," Elek replied, handing Lukács his refreshed glass. Lukács received it with unsteady hands. "So your parents prayed and submerged themselves deeper into their faith."

Elek returned to the sword, and again Lukács followed. Elek changed the subject. "Legend has it that Attila found the sword in a field. He picked it up as though it was made from tin. When he returned it to his village, no one else in the village could lift it – or even budge it. From that day on he was marked for greatness."

"I know the Prophet's history, Elek," Lukács said tersely.

Unoffended, Elek continued, "But there is another legend, one spoken… less openly. One that says the angel Carviel gave Attila the sword directly, revealing Attila as his son." Elek looked at Lukács, waiting for a response.

Lukács gripped the glass tight; his knuckles faded in colour. Then he whipped it against the stone wall, sending shards of glass and the remainder of his Glenfiddich everywhere.

"That is blasphemy, and I am sanctioned to kill you right now, right here," Lukács shouted.

Elek had anticipated that kind of response from Lukács; after all, he was a devout priest. "It's just an alternative legend, Lukács. Surely you have heard it before?" Elek defended, caution creeping down his spine.

"How dare you repeat that shit in this hallowed sanctuary! The Vezető will hear of this profanity."

A smile extended across Elek's face. "Ah, yes, your precious Mátyás. Ask him what his plan was for you and your troubled Anya?"

Lukács breathed heavily, uncertain if he should pounce on the old man or storm out of the room.

"Against my advice, your father went to Gergõ. He didn't hold the esteemed position of Vezető back then; he was simply a member of the Társadalom. They decided to end you and your mother Iren's life."

Lukács' mouth dried. *Lies, he is lying!*

"They realized your mother had gone through the *change*, and the hallucinations were actually *rememberings*. So, understandably, you also had to be eliminated. But, so far, and lucky for you, only the three of us knew about it. I mean, can you imagine the kind of ruin the KRÁJCÁR would go through if the membership found out that one of our own was a Nephilim – a son of the Testvériség, no less? It would have ripped the faith apart."

Reaching out blindly for the table to support himself, Lukács stumbled backwards into the chairs. He felt as if Elek had just punched him in the chest. He couldn't breathe. His mind raced and his eyes darted everywhere.

If this had happened before his assignment in Chile, he would have killed Elek right where he stood, gutting him with his knife and silencing his lying tongue with his own intestines. But his own visions, his own *remembering* of Lilith and Rabdebar, and other, more subtle experiences since then had damaged him; it had *changed* him. Hating himself for it was an understatement. He was raised by his mother to hate the very thing they themselves had become (what she always was). He had even trained to assassinate what he was, and he was good at it – shit, he even enjoyed it. But he knew what Elek was saying was the truth. Lukács dropped down on his hands and knees and vomited onto the floor. The room swayed and rocked like the deck of a boat on the high seas. His Anya's face flashed in front of him, and Lilith's haunting stare floated around his head. And then he recalled the scripture on the sword: *From One Comes Many.*

Even on his hands and knees, Lukács swayed. He tried to look up at Elek, to compose a little dignity, but his nausea forced him to look at his expensive loafer instead. The smell of his sick just inches from his face was bringing on another surge. Mercifully, everything went black and Lukács dropped to the floor.

"Get up!" Elek half ordered/half suggested and tossed a warm cloth down onto Lukács' face. After being struck by the damp cloth, Lukács opened his eyes. At first, all he could see was white until his heavy hand pulled the cloth off of his eyes. Lukács slumped into the chair and wiped his face. The stench of puke still filled the air and his mouth; the vomit was still pooled on the floor.

"Here, drink this," Elek said and handed him a glass filled with more whiskey. Lukács gave Elek a sideways look. *Fuck it,* he thought, and took a sip.

"So what happened next?" Lukács asked, his voice harsh and raspy. "Obviously we weren't killed."

"Mátyás agreed with me, but in doing so he made me swear to never challenge the second Vezető chair that rightfully belonged to my family. The plan was to commit your mother into a mental institution and watch over you very closely. But your father, Armand, disagreed. The two of you were an abomination in his eyes – no different than the thousands we have exterminated over the centuries. He planned to go to the Vezető, Gergõ's father, himself. So Gergõ and I told him that if we couldn't change his mind then we would stand by his side. Fortunately, the Vezető was away on business and he wouldn't be back for a day or so. That night your father stayed here in the palace, and Gergõ and I killed him in his bed and disposed of his body accordingly. We told your mother he found another girl downtown and left with her."

"You killed my father?"

"We saved your life. From that day on, Iren devoted even more of herself to Attila's teachings. Running from the humiliation of her husband abandoning her for another woman, and hiding from what she believed to be satanic visions, she became obsessed with the Holy Szentirás Magyar Bible," Elek said, looking above Lukács into space. "But how do you hide from what you are?" he said quietly, almost like an afterthought.

Lukács knew his mother's obsession wasn't normal, but that's what made her so saintly. "Did you have her killed too?" Lukács questioned, ready to strike Elek regardless of the consequences.

"No. The day she beat you – the last time she beat you and sent you to the hospital – I stopped by and talked with her. She told me that earlier in the day, before you came home from school, an angel had visited her right there in her home. She said it told her that the visions were not from Ha-Sata but from God, and that her son was fated for great things." Elek took a sip of whiskey. "She told me it was then and there that she realized the angel was Lucifer in disguise, and if the Prophet Attila allowed that to happen, then the Prophet had also abandoned her, like her husband. I told her *you* still lived and were recovering, and that you still needed her." Elek rotated the glass in his hand as he stared through the rusty drink. "She gave me a smile. Looking back on it now, it was a weak smile. She said she would like to visit you in the hospital if I'd come back in the morning to get her. She said she needed to get some of your things ready. She hung herself that night in the kitchen, by the table. That's when you came to live with us."

Elek took another sip and swallowed it down hard. The memory of walking in and seeing her body hanging exactly where she stood when she said goodbye to him the evening before was difficult for him. He had handed out a lot of assignments to the Testvériség to eliminate the very same kind of people as her, but he had never actually done an assignment himself, and he had never known any of the victims. The idea of killing people that were already tormented, who by no action of their own were targeted and killed by his organization, never again sat right with him. Iren was a good woman, a devoted Attilian, and a loyal Hungarian. She was the embodiment of everything the KRÁJCÁR stood for and protected, and even more so than anybody knew.

Lukács lifted his hands to his face and heavily sobbed into them. He cried for losing a father he never knew, he cried for losing his Anya, and he cried because he had never gone to her funeral (if she even had one). He never got to say goodbye. But more so, he cried now because in the last twenty-four years he had never cried at all. He became a hard, callous soldier who only needed the next assignment; it was an obsession equal only to his mother's.

After several long moments, Lukács wiped his face with the damp cloth and regained some composure. "How is it possible? How can I...? How can my mother...?" Lukács couldn't find the will to say the words.

"Attila," Elek interjected.

"What?" Lukács' body felt heavy and weighted down as he pushed himself up onto his feet.

"Attila," Elek repeated, and turned towards the Sword of God. "You see, Lukács, angelic swords cannot be used by just anyone; it can only be used by the angel who created it, or... by its heir. I understand it was incredibly difficult to even place the sword up here on these golden hands – the Hands of God, as someone once told me. The archives describe how it took five men with a block and tackle and chain to raise it up onto these palms. I guess, physically, the sword only weighs a few kilograms and the Hands of God can easily support it, but once you apply *personal intention* to it, like wanting to pick it up and take it home, or wanting to use it in battle, its weight becomes colossal. Once you remove your intention, it once again only weighs a few kilograms."

Lukács gained back some strength in his legs. "Are you saying the prophet was a Nephilim? That is still blasphemy," he charged, but his voice was low, his fighting spirit not fully returned.

"I wasn't the first to make that claim. When Attila was the only person who could wield the sword, the Huns claimed him to be their ruler – their *King Arthur*, so to speak. When Carviel instructed Attila to rid the world of the Angelic Script and destroy every person who possessed the Knowledge, the Hun tribes united in even greater numbers. With his new divine objective, Attila created the KRÁJCÁR. It became his very own Crusades. The Romans told their citizens that we were murderers, barbarians. Somehow that became accepted history. "

"What does this have to do with my Anya?" Lukács demanded, a little more of the fight returning to him.

"After several years of battle, Attila had bedded hundreds – perhaps thousands – of women along the invasion route, as was common back then. But as the years carried on, his older brother, Bleda, noticed that every one of his offspring were daughters."

"That's not true," Lukács interrupted. "He had three sons: Ellak, Dengizik, and Ernak."

Elek let slip a guffaw, "Surely you don't believe Attila's wife was any more faithful than he was? Women get lonely too. Some say they were more his nephews than his sons." He continued with his story, "Bleda concluded that Attila could only produce daughters, and that Attila himself was an *angyal fia*, or 'son of an angel.' I can only imagine what Bleda thought about his own mother at that moment; I am sure it put a new spin on sibling rivalry. But it makes perfect sense: he was the only one who could wield the *Isten Kardja*, and we can't overlook the Hun's *supernatural* success."

"Of course it was supernatural; he was a prophet. He was guided by the hand of God," Lukács interrupted again.

"It was more than prophetic intuition. Think about it, when Attila inherited his position from his father, he brought together tribes of nomads and gypsies against one of the most powerful empires in human history, the Romans, and made them pay – a lot. Anyway, Bleda brought his suspicions to Attila's three sons. The sons weren't worried that their father was the very monster they were sanctioned to eliminate; instead, they realized that this new information threatened their inheritance of his throne and their birth right to rule the Huns after Attila's death.

One night in 445 A.D., Bleda mysteriously died. History is very vague about his death, and even the Társadalom records hold almost nothing on it. That same year, the three sons convinced their father to commission the Group of Thirteen, an elite membership of the Huns' most noble families, to lead the KRÁJCÁR in its virtuous quest to purge the Knowledge. Attila liked the idea, but Ellak, Dengizik, and Ernak had other reasons for its ordination – they wanted to scour all of the villages and tribes throughout their conquest and 'remove' all of Attila's illegitimate children.

The Group of Thirteen retraced the continent, hitting all of the towns and villages that Attila and his men had liberated, killing every woman and every daughter under nineteen. But, as you can attest to in your own career, the scope and magnitude of such a quest was too great for a mere thirteen individuals. The percentages were not in their favour, so the Thirteen created the Társadalom as the administrators to oversee the internal workings of the organization, and the Testvériség as its sword out in the field. Still, many were missed – perhaps some were married off to a new tribe, or were simply out of town when the Thirteen came riding through. Anyway, the women that were missed," Elek raised his hand, gesturing to Lukács, "had children."

Lukács stared down at the floor, his eyes following the swirls and patterns in the black and gold carpet. His mind sluggishly tried to process all this new information while his emotions tried to distract him from it. Then he smiled a crooked smile.

"Oh, I see, I've got it. You're telling me all this shit about my parents... my dad was a funny guy and I would have liked him, but too bad he wanted me and my mother dead. And my mom was a great gal, but too bad she was mentally insane and, oh – half Nephilim – was it?"

Lukács raised his eyes and stared into Elek's. Rage burned behind his pupils. "And not only does that make me the same fucking abomination I've been hunting all these years, but I am also supposed to believe that I am the heir of Attila?"

Lukács charged at Elek, grabbing him by the lapels of his suit jacket, and marched him backwards until he slammed him hard against the wall. Elek tried to give Lukács the time he needed to process the facts, but a nervous smile was clearly visible on his face. Lukács exhaled heavily, no longer interested in containing his anger. Drops of spittle hung from his lower lip.

"You are a liar and a dead man. Did you honestly believe bringing up stories and accusations about my parents was going to delay my report to the Vezető? Did you think your silver tongue was going to distract me? Did you think by integrating me into your elaborate fantasy I would need to keep MY MOUTH SHUT?"

Lukács again slammed Elek against the wall. His face was so close to Elek's that they were breathing the same air. Elek stayed strong and defiant. Lukács could easily rip him apart if he decided to – after all, that is what he was trained to do. But the fact that Lukács hadn't yet harmed him meant that something he said to Lukács had touched a button inside of him. Something was taming this dog – a truth somewhere that Lukács already knew or was coming to realize.

Although Elek was physically pinned to the wall by the Hungarian assassin, his mind replayed the evening from when he met Lukács in the briefing room until now. Elek looked down at the duffle bag that was still slightly visible under the table. Then he fixed his eyes back on Lukács. "The scrolls!" Elek declared. Lukács blinked with surprise at Elek's intuition. "Why did you disobey a direct order from Mátyás and keep the scrolls?"

Lukács' grip weakened and his hands slid off of Elek's jacket. Elek was somehow piecing together Lukács' new dark secret, and as he watched the cogs working away behind Elek's eyes, his own rage drained out of him.

"What would cause the great Lukács Vadász to disobey?" Elek thought out loud.

Elek stood taller and leaned away from the wall, growing more confident. At the same time, Lukács stepped back from him. "Something happened to you when you touched the scrolls, didn't it? You had a vision," Elek both questioned and stated.

Lukács looked back at the bag and Lilith's face returned to him. Elek had somehow figured it out. He felt instantly lighter as the weight from hiding the secret lifted off of him, but the relief was fleeting and short-lived as the consequence of the secret pressed its own weight down.

"It wasn't a vision," Lukács stammered. He could no longer look up at Elek. "It was a hallucination."

Elek smiled. He more than smiled: he beamed. His face lit up with the intensity of a man holding a winning lottery ticket. He was right. After decades of research into Attila's past, and even more years of assumptions about Lukács', he was right.

"It is okay son. It is all right. Your secret is safe with me... for now."

"FOR NOW!" Lukács fired back. Being cornered had reset his *fight or flight* instinct. "I have no secret. I had a breakdown – that is all. Better yet, I'll have nothing to hide if I kill you."

Elek's winning smile resumed its nervousness. "Listen, Lukács, you are the heir of Attila the Hun: a living, breathing connection to our beloved Prophet. You have no one to fear. Embrace your destiny. You, Lukács, should be sitting at the head of the KRÁJCÁR. Sitting right there," Elek pointed to Gergõ's chair, "as Vezető."

Lukács' eyes betrayed him as he followed Elek's finger to the large oak table. His world was spinning out of control. His life had completely flipped around in less than 24 hours.

"So what am I supposed to do, Elek? Walk into the next meeting and proclaim my heritage? Tell them I am taking the Vezető position and they should all just understand?" He mocked the conversation they would have: "'And why do you think you should be Vezető, Lukács?' 'Well, Gergõ, I can't prove it but Elek says I am the Prophet's great, great grandson or thereabouts. And it just made sense to me and you should believe him. Please.' I don't think that would go well for me," Lukács spat bitterly.

"It would if you were holding the sword," Elek replied. He held the glass of whiskey just inches from his lips, taking in its full, distinct aroma and studying Lukács' body language.

At its mere suggestion, Lukács eyed the angelic sword resting on the Hands of God. He could feel the sword beckoning him to give it a try – the golden palms an extension of the sword's own desire for Lukács' embrace. *Come to me, Lukács. Take me. I belong to you.*

Who was he to think that he deserved the honour to wield the *Isten Kardja*, Lord Attila's holy rapier? It was a religious artifact, a physical and tangible piece of history he only moments ago believed was lost to the world. Lukács wasn't righteous enough to touch the sword or make any claim to it. Even the thought of such a bold act left guilt on the tip of his tongue, giving him a bad taste. But... but...what if? What if Elek was telling the truth? Even if only some of his story was true. What if his Anya's vision – the visions she used the Magyar Bible to hide from – were the same visions he had in Chile? Did she see Lilith and her penetrating eyes? Did she hallucinate golden cloud cities like the ones he had seen while flying across the United States and Europe?

Again the sword beckoned him. *Come to me, Son of Carviel, seed of Attila.*

The spot lights blaring down over the sword gave the gleaming gold fingers the appearance of stretching out towards him, reaching for him. He was beginning to doubt his place within the Testvériség now. Should he take the seat of Vezető? Could he? Was it right? The sword felt like it belonged to him, even though he had not yet touched it.

Come to me.

"Go to it," Elek said, reading the internal conflict on his troubled face.

Hold me.

"Hold it," Elek pushed, as if he was mocking the sword's own taunts.

Lukács took a step forward, transfixed on the shimmering, glistening blade. His mind floated above his body. His eyes reread the inscription.

“What does ‘From One Comes Many’ mean?” he asked, mostly to himself and almost expecting the sword to answer him.

“That’s what is written on the sword, isn’t it? You can read it?” Elek smiled wider than he had ever smiled before, and his eyes bulged in their sockets. He was right. He knew it. There remained no question now as to Lukács’ lineage, or about his destiny.

“Take the sword, Lukács. Take it and claim your seat as Vezető.” The adrenaline pumped through Elek’s body and vibrated the glass of scotch whiskey out of his hand, feeding what was left of his drink to the carpet at his feet.

Lukács took another step closer to the sword and another until he stood only centimeters from it. The golden finger tips brushed his pants. He looked down at it, his body numb, and his arms leadened at his sides. He continued to watch himself from above, outside of his own body, as his right hand cautiously reached out and gently caressed the golden fingers that offered up the angelic blade. He found he was afraid to touch it. He was afraid to discover the truth – not that he was the true heir of Attila, but that he wasn’t. He was afraid to find out that his mother was truly psychotic, and so was he. He had the opportunity right now to walk away, to never know. Perhaps some doors were meant to be left closed, and some secrets kept secret.

Elek held his breath as he watched the assassin priest hesitate in front of the sword. He watched Lukács caress the golden fingers, afraid to cross the the cm gap to the sword itself. Truth of oneself can be enlightening, freeing, but more often than not it is only a great disappointment. Lukács was battling nothing less than his own identity, with who he knew he was (or believed himself to be), and how much he was willing to give to allow that to change.

Elek too was gambling. If Lukács could wield the Sword of God then he would sit second seat to the most powerful man in the most powerful organization on the planet. But if Lukács reached for the sword and couldn't wield it, then he would surely lose everything, including his life.

Lukács couldn't remember being afraid of anything in his adult life, but this – this little movement of his hand muscles – paralyzed him with fear. He knew now he couldn't go back. There was no walking away from the sword. He was going to reach out and claim the destiny that awaited him, either as the KRÁJCÁR's new Vezető, or its humble servant. But his fingers wanted to punish him first by making him wait. Lukács could only move them at their discretion. *This is your future too,* he said mentally to his hand. *Let's get on with it.*

Elek watched Lukács move closer into the sword. Lukács' hand reached out and his fingers curled around the handle. Then his body straightened and tightened as though the sword was somehow electrocuting him. His head inched back, pushing his face up towards the alcove ceiling, and his mouth stretched open in a voiceless scream.

Elek didn't know if he should move in closer to Lukács or run for his life. All he could do was stare at Lukács and hold his breath.

Lukács knew as soon as his fingers touched the rapier that he was meant for it. This wasn't Attila's sword; it was his! Energy coursed through his fingers, up his arm, through is chest, and into his mind.

Lukács watched through the young Attila's eyes as the angel Carviel handed him the rapier on the ancient grounds of the Hungarian plains. He saw the battles and the conquests of the Huns through the eyes of the Prophet. He heard Attila's words to his men, and his shouts to the Romans. He felt Attila's heart beat; Lukács now knew the blood that pumped through Attila's veins was the same blood that ran through his own. Lukács then felt the Prophet's lusts become his own until finally their thoughts merged.

Lukács' knuckles turned white as he gripped the sword tighter and lifted it off of the golden hands. Elek stumbled back both shocked and exhilarated. It was all happening – everything he ever wanted, everything he ever dreamed about was coming true. The KRÁJCÁR had changed – Gergõ Mátyás just didn't know it yet – and Elek couldn't wait to see his face when Lukács held the Sword of God in front of him.

Elek quickly knelt down on one knee. "Vezető!"

CHAPTER THIRTY-NINE

"I know what you are thinking about doing Curtis," Eavery said, appearing suddenly in the kitchen doorway. "The Parcae have woven your fate; it cannot be undone."

Curtis looked at the Sumerian god the way someone might look at a homeless drug addict.

"I understand what you are going through. I have lost everyone I have ever cared for," Eavery confessed, his voice thick and sad. "I have been utterly alone for 3 thousand years, with occasional breaks of friendship – like the one I now have with you. But after your death, after you have died from old age or in some mortal combat somewhere, I will carry-on, alone again. The Parcae have also woven my fate as they do for both gods and mortals, but unfortunately, as a god, I can read their tapestry; I know my ending. Believe me, it is something you cannot rewrite."

Curtis couldn't hear him. He couldn't hear the warnings and advice Eavery was trying to give, and he wouldn't hear the sorrow of someone else's pain. Maybe, deep down inside, Curtis felt pity for his friend, and perhaps he would even tell him so after he has his own family back by his side. Maybe, someday, he would put an arm over Eavery's shoulder and listen to his friend's stories, raise a pint of ale, and toast to his pain. But not now. Not today. Now, he was going to rewind the past to just before the moment Vivica was killed on the plateau.

"Instead of telling her to run away with Charlie, I can just '*pop*' them both back here," he muttered to himself, his mind whirling away with possibilities and his ears closed to anything else.

"Curtis, you can't change what has been written. Even the gods are at the mercy of the Fates," Eavery's voice was loud and desperate.

"I can rewind the last three days back to when I had them both in my arms and bring them back here and then pop back to the plateau and kill that bitch," Curtis fired back, his voice louder and more desperate. How dare an ancient ghost tell him that he couldn't go back to save his family!

Curtis walked passed Eavery and into the living room. "How dare you..." Curtis spat out, his words venomous and bitter. "How dare you try to prevent me from saving my family, my Charlie." Curtis paced back and forth. "You bring up some bullshit about witches controlling my fate – maybe back in your day, but not anymore, not with me." Curtis stopped and squared off with Eavery, his wings spread out wide like the tail feathers of a peacock and the black sword in his hand. "In case you haven't noticed, *pal*, I'm the new god on the block. I have seen the creation of the earth. I have looked down on Eden. I have witnessed Satan being tossed out of Heaven. I can manipulate time. I am more than *I was* and I am more than *you are*."

Eavery stepped closer. "Curtis, please, don't do this. Don't witness your family's death again."

"I won't, Eavery, I will see them alive," Curtis smiled and gave him a wink.

To Eavery it looked as though Curtis just stopped moving – as if he simply froze in place. In the next second, Curtis blinked out of existence. Then he was back slobbering over his wife's picture, again a broken man. Because Eavery was a god, time moved around him differently.

Curtis looked up, "Why weren't you there? You could have helped me save them. You're a fucking god – why didn't you help me?"

Eavery couldn't stand to see his friend crushed again. He walked past Curtis sitting on the sofa. Again, he passed through the large living room windows and blasted the thick curtains aside to flood the room in blinding sun light. His heart was heavy with sorrow for his friend.

A thousand times Curtis came back, and a thousand times Eavery watched him freeze in place and blink out of existence to try to save his family. It was an infinite loop of trial and error. Each time Curtis returned, he came back a little less like himself and a little more like a twisted, desperate man. He couldn't remember any of the previous attempts he made to change the past, but his soul did, and it was scarred and disfigured by each failure.

"Curtis, please don't try it again. You can't bring them back," Eavery pleaded.

"What, I have tried to save them before?" Curtis could barely hold his head up, his eyes sunken and black.

Eavery felt for his friend deeply. "Yes, and every time you have failed."

"But I don't remember any of it," Curtis said, his wings heavy as if he stored all of his guilt within the feathers.

"That is because seconds after you return to the past, your future is pulled from you. Your past becomes your present and you lose the knowledge of what is to come next. You could go back another thousand times, but Vivica and Charlie will always die on the plateau on the night of the Summer Solstice. Their fates have already been written."

A sense of calm came over Curtis.

"That's it!" he shouted, lifting his sword. "That's it! I need to go back farther. I need to go back before she leaves for Ireland, before I left for Israel. If I never go to Israel and she never leaves for Ireland, our lives never get tangled up in all of this shit."

Before Eavery could reply, Curtis was gone.

***

Beep! Beep! Beep!

The clock on the nightstand flashed 5:05 AM as the alarm filled the bedroom. Curtis blinked heavily and slapped at the clock.

"Getting up? It's your turn to take Charlie to daycare," Vivica said from under the covers. Curtis bolted upright and quickly looked around the room. It wasn't a dark and eerie plateau. There was no golden ring, no Jacob's Ladder, and no bitch trying to kill his family – he did it! He went back to the morning before he ever heard about the exercise in Israel. Curtis snuggled deeper into the covers and up against Vivica.

"Aren't you getting up... going to work?" she muffled from somewhere under the pillow.

"Nah! I'm calling in sick. Let's keep Charlie home today. We can have a happy Papp family day. What do you say?"Vivica let out a *'mmph'* and fell back to sleep. Sphinx, on the other hand, let out a hungry meow from the foot of the bed.

Curtis looked over his shoulder. "Hungry? I couldn't sleep either. Let's go and wake up Charlie, and then I will get you some food."

Curtis kissed the pillow somewhere above Vivica's head and floated out of the bedroom, feeling lighter than he had in years. He watched Charlie's rhythmic breathing. She was clutching her pink blanket, still deep in sleep. He couldn't help but study her beautiful face: her long, curved eyelashes, her tiny, delicate nose, her four year old lips that were comically flexing and jutting – no doubt she was having a conversation with *Dora the Explorer* or one of the *Imagination Movers* somewhere in dream land. With Charlie's breathing, Vivica's muffled snoring, and Sphinx's purring, Curtis was the happiest he could ever remember being.

This should never change – will never change, he thought to himself. *I will make all different choices to ensure this never changes.*

Curtis looked at his arm and traced the red and black serpent tattoo with his eyes. The sight of the snake startled him; he was afraid to move his arm on the chance that the serpent might strike. He couldn't remember ever getting that tattoo, and why in hell did he ever pick such a hideous one! Before his eyes, the snake's open mouth and scaly form faded from his skin until his arm was as it always had been – plain. As the tattoo faded, Curtis couldn't believe his eyes. Then, just as quickly, the memory of ever having witnessed his dissolving tattoo also faded.

Curtis blinked once, twice, and then looked down at the cat. "Want some food?" he whispered. "I need some coffee."

The following Monday, Curtis logged onto his work computer and waited for it to load up his profile. Sergeant O'Connell walked into the lab holding his stainless steel coffee mug.

"Feeling better?" O'Connell asked, taking a seat at the work bench.

"Yeah," Curtis meekly replied. "Thanks for getting Granier to fill in for me, I don't know what came over me – we all felt pretty shitty this weekend." Curtis remembered lying to Sarge about not feeling good, but he couldn't remember *why* he lied.

"No problem. I guess it was all a bust anyway. The whole thing got squashed before it even started – called the troops back home due to some Israeli activity in the Mediterranean. Granier just did some sightseeing. He will be in later to sign his leave pass; we're giving him a couple days of vacation for his trouble."

As if right on cue, Cpl. Granier stepped into the lab. Dressed in sandals, shorts, and a floral Hawaiian shirt, he walked up to Curtis' desk. He was still wide awake from the flight back and wired on energy drinks.

"Man, did you miss a good time! The flight out sucked, but I hit the links with a couple of German chicks – Search and Rescue Techs doing desert training. Man, could those Germans drink! They couldn't play golf worth a shit, but who cares – they were hot. Hey Sarge didn't see you there.

Here's my leave pass," Granier rattled out in one breath. Curtis and Sgt. O'Connell smirked to each other.

"You're here early; I expected you in later to get this signed," Sarge remarked, taking the leave pass from him.

"Oh, yeah, couldn't sleep man. Partied the whole way back. The plane was jumping. We had free drinks. Even the Major was looped." Granier looked down at the pass and back up at Sarge. "You gonna sign that?"

"Yes, Richard, let me check it first – make sure the dates are good." Sgt. O'Connell rolled his eyes.

Granier looked back at Curtis who was bobbing his head to the beat of some internal song.

"Cool picture, man. It's creepy though. Did Charlie draw that?" he motioned with his nose at a drawing taped to the wall beside Curtis' computer.

"That, yeah, she just drew that for me this morning before I brought her to daycare. What an imagination that girl has. She said that these three witches control everybody's lives, but if you look closely, there are faint black lines attached to their feet and hands like marionette's strings, and they in turn are controlled by this guy in a black hood. She even had me write in their names under them: Nona, Decima, and Morta," Curtis said through a smile, still impressed with his daughter's imagination.

"It's true man. Everyone's got a boss," Granier said matter-of-factly. "Oh, I almost forgot, I got something for you." Granier fidgeted through his pockets, pulling items out and placing them on Curtis' desk: gum, a golf card, keys, a condom still in its package. "Oops, I'll just put that away."

"Not used?" Curtis sniggered.

“Partied too hard… passed out,” Granier returned, not slowing in his search. “Here it is,” he said, handing Curtis a small stone figurine. Curtis took the stone doll and rotated it in his hand.

“Nope, not that,” Granier said, taking it back from him. “I picked that up in a store in Nevatim for Clyde’s kid; I heard he’s into that kind of stuff. This here,” he said fishing out a small bag of sand and dropped it with the other stuff on the desk.

“What’s this?” Curtis asked, smirking at the gift and poking at it with his finger.

“It’s a little bit of Israel for you at home, man. You know, since you couldn’t make it. This lady on a corner was selling it for about 25 cents. I didn’t want it but she persuaded me, said I should bring a little bit of the Holy Land back to Canada for my friends.”

“Really? She swept dust off the side walk and you paid for it?” Sarge jumped in, laughing.

“No… I don’t think so, man. She was very nice – smelled like apples – said it was sand from some holy site somewhere. I don’t know why, but I just had to bring it back and give it to you.”

CHAPTER FORTY

3 months later
Dartmouth, Nova Scotia

Robert Pulman watched as the teenage girls, dressed in short skirts, exited the Dartmouth Public High School. *Slim. Petite. Young. Perfect.*

Robert Pulman was neither young, nor slim. His forty-something frame was sixty pounds heavier than his swollen ankles could manage on a daily basis, causing chronic pain and a morning routine of 400mg acetaminophen with his three cups of coffee. But he was successful. His Tag Heuer Calibre S wristwatch was proudly mounted and displayed prominently, if not forcefully, around his plump left wrist said so (if one was so shallow as to notice). His clothing attire, on the other hand, narrated a different depiction of the short, large man. He wore 1950s-style white and black patent leather shoes, cuffed, baggy designer jeans, which occasionally displayed his dark and hairy ass cleavage, and a black and white-striped and collard dress shirt, buttoned most of the way up but still displaying a canopy of dark hair that forested his chest and back.

His left hand no longer betrayed him with a tan-less ring on his finger – his divorce was finalized back in May because his wife (ex-wife) couldn't handle the success of his photography career. Her insecurity of him taking pictures of beautiful, young models was something she needed to deal with but couldn't. He was an *artist*, damn it! Plus, he made excellent money. And if he received the occasional hand job or blow job, so what? It meant nothing. And sometimes it was hard not to get caught up in the moment. It didn't matter that he was getting more action now than when he was married.

His thick lips slid apart, exposing his bleached white teeth as he intercepted a teenage cheerleader texting on her iPhone.

“Excuse me,” Robert said as he stepped in front of her. “Excuse me,” he said again, suppressing his annoyance with teenagers and their addiction to their cell phones.

April Murphy looked up from her texting and brightly smiled at the hairy, fat man that looked like he just stepped out of an Old Navy commercial.

“Is this Dartmouth Public High School?” Robert asked, pointing to the brown, bricked building that displayed a large sign announcing “Dartmouth Public High School” in gold lettering.

“Yes it is,” April said, still smiling, not wanting to be impolite but eager to get back to texting Joanie, her *BFF*.

“Is the school office still open? I need to post some fliers for a photo shoot.”*10... 9... 8...* Robert counted in his head.

“Photo shoot? For what?”

Robert’s smile widened past another bleached tooth. With the ease and grace of a snake in water – the kind of ease and grace that only comes with repetition – he slid out a black, leather card holder from his breast pocket and pulled out a business card. “PPP Pulman Professional Photography” was stamped in silver lettering on a black card.

“I am looking for young, fit models – both men and women – it doesn’t matter to me. I use both to put a human face on internet sites. It pays about $200 an hour.” *7... 6... 5...*

“$200 an hour? What kind of sites?”

“Well, sometimes they are vacation sites: *Sandals,* for instance. And for that I’ll need models dressed in a bikini or swim trunks enjoying the beach. Other times it may be for a department store, and I’ll need someone young and hip to model clothes. This particular one is a small contract so I don’t need many models. Do you know of anyone who...

might be interested? It would save me a walk up to the office."*4... 3... 2...*

"$200 an hour? For how long?"

Robert watched April's eyes bounce from the business card she was bending and rolling in her hands to the other students (or competition) passing by. He knew she was imagining how to spend the quick cash at the mall. Robert could tell what was going on in her pretty little head; he had seen it dozens of times.

"For an hour, maybe two, depending on how it goes." Robert could almost read her thoughts. Four hundred dollars can buy a lot of... whatever a seventeen year old buys today. He leaned back and gave her a scrutinizing look up and down.

"Your hair is pretty white. Are you a natural blonde or do you bleach your hair?"

"No, it's my natural colour," April said, almost offended by his abruptness.

Indeed, she would take some good pictures. You can always make more on the albinos – especially the young ones. Now he needed to close the deal before she could rationalize how unorthodox this really was. Today's teenagers are far savvier about the world than he was at their age, but they are still *teenagers*, day-dreaming of instant fame and celebrity through miracles and happenstance.

"You can keep the card. I need to head up to the school's office before they close."

It never seemed to matter that he wasn't holding a single poster or flier, but then again, in the last five years, he had never had to get to the school's office.

As April watched Robert walk around her and begin to head up the sidewalk, she felt an unbelievable opportunity begin to slip past her. April reached out and touched his arm, stopping him beside her.

"What would I be modeling… if you think you might want me?"

And one…, Robert thought – he had her. "This particular contract is for lingerie." This young cheerleader had already made up her mind, but he liked to give them something to make their decisions a little more palatable – a small lie to help the medicine go down, sort of thing. "Paris Hilton is creating a new line of lingerie and it will be debuting in Canada by the end of summer."

Of course this was a complete fabrication. The photos were going to be part of a variety of internet advertisements for penis enlargements, porn sites, and spam emails, but when you drop a phrase like, "Paris Hilton is creating a new line… *for anything*," common sense is fantasized out of the *target's* eyes. And that is how he saw them – as targets. Targets for money and targets for sex.

"Listen," Robert said, his tone slithering from businessman to compassionate agent, "if you want to bring along a friend, I might be able to use her, but you will have to split the pay cheque."

"When do you want to do the photo shoot?" April asked, feeling a little selfish with her good fortune.

"The sooner we get done, the sooner I send them in. Get a jump on the competition – you know what I mean?"

"Yeah," she said and slipped her iPhone into her purse.

Whew! Robert thought to himself. *First I said it was a contract, and now it's a competition. You're slipping, Pulman.*

It didn't matter. April never noticed she was being manipulated and guided through the dance (as Robert liked to think of it), and that too was how Robert saw it – as a dance. Every new city was a new song with a new dance partner.

"Good, we can do our shoot now and you'll be home for supper two – maybe three – hundred dollars richer. Perhaps even with a modeling career to boot. Make mom and dad proud."

"I don't know about that. I never met my dad and my mother hardly spoke of him. But she's dead now, my mom. She was killed at a bus stop for her cigarettes. I live with my godparents now."

Sorry I asked. This chick is a basket case. "Do you need a ride?"

"No, I have a car."

"Great. Boy these summers are chilly out here," he said and fastened up the top button on his shirt. "Meet me at the Sea Side Inn on Ocean View Road, room two-oh-nine." Robert turned and headed back down the sidewalk to his car. Proud of himself, a hard-on was already beginning to form in his briefs.

"Mr. Pulman, don't forget your dog," April called after him, pointing to a mangy black mutt off in the grass.

"What?" Robert turned and saw the scruffy fur ball. "That's not mine," he sneered and kept on walking.

***

Sea Side Inn, Room 209

Robert Pulman tacked three 8x8 feet satin sheets up on the wall behind the bed and sofa, covering the generic portraits and wall designs that were all too common in hotel chains. For less than a hundred dollars, he turned a cheap hotel room into an even cheaper studio. He casually tossed half a dozen magazines of *ELLE, GLAMOUR,* and *Teen Vogue,* all with beautiful young girls with modeling careers smiling on the front covers. Robert hadn't actually taken any of the pictures displayed on the covers, or even any of the pictures throughout the magazines, but if this new, young dance partner of his – April *something* – mistakenly got that perception, then oh well. He pushed and twisted a bottle of seven dollar sparkling wine deeper into the plastic ice bucket. "A little drink to help relax the budding model," he scoffed out loud in the empty room.

He looked over at the selection of dresses and lingerie he had hanging on a rolling costume trolley. Two years earlier while vacationing in Indonesia, Robert had made an investment in a labeling machine that significantly bolstered his business and consequently his sex life. Initially, it was a standard labeler that stitched thread onto cloth to personalize pillow cases or underwear, but when combined with an image scanner and proper software (which he also purchased in Indonesia), Robert could duplicate any designer label on the market. He even created a few of his own. Talking young girls into modeling for an 'up and coming' Japanese designer ready to break into the market was a lot like taking candy from a baby.

Robert checked the labels again on his three favourite teddies to ensure the stitching was holding. He slid his sausage-like fingers over the crotch of the pink teddy in front, caressing it between his thumb and forefinger. The mere thought of April's toned, young frame pressing and moving against the delicate rayon fabric caused his penis to swell and rise up the left side of his thigh. He could hardly wait.

Three soft taps came from the hallway door. "Mr. Pulman?" a voice barely whispered from the other side. At the sound of her voice Robert's heart rate instantly sped up and he could feel his blood pressure increase throughout his bell-shaped body. His skin flushed red as it always did when he got excited.

Robert released the supple material. "Coming!" he called out to the door. *And so will you*, he said to himself and repositioned the bulge in his pants.

On his way by he cracked open the case to his NIKON D3s camera. Peering through the peep hole he checked to see if the seventeen year old cheerleader *slash* model was alone and not accompanied by any friends (perhaps wearing a black uniform and sporting a badge). He ogled her through the distorted lens for a half second longer. He checked his repositioned bulge and opened the door.

"Come in, come in, April, I am glad you came," Robert said, using his non-threatening let's get down to business voice.

As April stepped out of the hallway and into the room her instincts were screaming, telling her that something was definitely wrong. But April had led a fairly sheltered life, and until today she had never needed her instincts. She had never before been placed in a position to learn the language of her inner voice. But she was about to.

CHAPTER FORTY-ONE

As April walked past the obese "Ritchie Cunningham" she heard him inhale, smelling her. April knew she aroused Robert Pulman – women can always tell. She didn't need his red flushed face or his excessively wide smile to tell her that. Women are trained in their grade school years to read the signs from the hockey players or gym teachers.

She looked around the room and noticed the clothes on the rack first, and then the sheets on the walls, the magazines, the bottle of *Champagne*, and finally the camera.

I might actually go through with this, she thought, still blind to the magnitude of the scenario unfolding around her, but not blind to the sleazy sideways glances from the photographer.

"Go ahead and take a look at the clothes. I pegged you as a size ONE so I put the other sizes away," he said as he dropped a closed envelope with one hundred and eighty-five dollars beside the camera case. He took extended stares at her legs and ass, believing all along she didn't notice and that he was getting away with it.

As she examined the delicate garments, Robert pulled out a fifteen-page document of small typed legalese stating he was the sole proprietor of all photos taken on this date (and possible future dates), and that she was at the minimum age of eighteen (which of course he was sure she wasn't, but never asked). All fifteen pages contained absurdly large words within convoluted and confusing paragraphs.

"I will need you to sign these legal papers before we can send your pics to Paris' people for review. I wanna protect your rights as a professional model and mine as your photographer. Those snakes in LA will try to take advantage of whoever they can. But before that, let's have a drink. You do like Champagne, don't you?"

"Champagne?" April echoed, her eyes twinkled and a smile curled under her lips. "I have never had champagne during the day before."

Using the hotel's hand towel, Robert popped the cork and poured two flutes of the sparkling wine.

"Well, you better get used to it," he said as he handed her the glass.

He made a toast to "world tours and exotic locations," as he had done many times in the past to other wannabe models. It still surprised him that such a vague and corny line worked. It had never mattered to them that they were in a cheap motel drinking cheap wine; he always saw visions of fame and glamour flash in their eyes – their imaginations were no doubt creating scenes of runways in Madrid, beach shots in Hawaii, and dance clubs in London. It didn't matter if they were young girls or young men; he teased and tickled their dreams with loaded phrases like: "better get used to it," "it's just the beginning," "you are going to blow them away," and, his favourite, "what country would you like to shoot in next?"

April's excitement was beginning to get the better of her. It was all feeling *so* real. Sure, the location was sleazy, but even Kate Moss had to have started at the bottom somewhere and look at her now – world famous, rich, flying around in expensive jets.

The champagne tasted dry and bitter on April's tongue, but she suppressed the urge to make a face. Instead, April tipped up the flute and emptied the wine down her throat. In an instant, Robert refilled her glass.

"There, once you are done with that, we need you to sign these papers. Then take an outfit off the rack and go change in the washroom."

April quickly emptied her glass again and picked up the large contract. She skimmed over the paragraphs of small, fine print and did her best to look like she understood what she was reading – even though she had no idea.

Robert enjoyed watching them pretend they knew what they were reading – it was obvious they didn't, or they never would have signed it in the first place. He let her play "adult" for another page and then hurried things along by paraphrasing each section and X-ing where she should initial and where she should sign her name in full.

Finally, Robert thought, *let's get down to business.*

Not waiting for the young teenager to choose, Robert strutted over to the rack and plucked off the teddy he was caressing earlier.

"Here, let's start with this one and see where that takes us."

"Whew!" April said, grabbing hold of the garment. "This is really going to happen."

"The first outfit is always the hardest. Do you want to smoke a joint to relax you?"

April blinked with surprise. "No, thank you."

"I don't like them either," Robert quickly lied. "But if that was your thing..."

As April stepped inside the washroom and closed the door, Robert quickly searched a hidden compartment in his camera case. A small Ziploc bag with a dozen blue pills and a tube of peppermint flavoured lube were inside. He swallowed the Viagra, unzipped his pants and began rubbing his swelling penis with the flavoured lube.

Better stop before it's too late, he cautioned himself. *My excitement might get the better of me.* Returning the lube back to the compartment, he buttoned his pants back up and licked the peppermint flavouring off his fingers and palm.

In the washroom, April slipped into the outfit and told herself that it wasn't *really* that much less fabric than her bikini. Flashes of the fame and dream dates with movie stars dimmed as the stale air of the hotel room hit her skin. In the mirror, she examined and repositioned the thong and scrutinized the shear fabric around her breasts. This wasn't the first time she'd worn a teddy – in fact, she owns a similar one hidden in her closet at home (for Troy, her boyfriend) – but now the world was going to see her in one. *How is Troy going to feel about that?*

Standing almost naked in front of a mirror, in a cheap hotel, April began to hear a tiny instinctive voice telling her that something was not right. But as April was beginning to acknowledge the sprouting cautionary voice in her head, the 17% alcohol in the sparkling wine began to silence it and dull her senses. With her head now swimming, she looked down and flipped through the pages of the La Senza flyer sitting on the small bathroom counter.

As her sense of adventure returned, so did April's courage. When she exited the washroom, the short, fat photographer was licking the fingers of his one hand and readjusting the fly of his pants with the other.

April quickly gulped down her refilled glass and sat on the bed. Finally seeing the teenage cheerleader in the teddy quickened Robert's heart rate further. He could feel his face redden again and his penis harden even more. *I might not have needed that Viagra.*

Robert had April whirl wind around the bed, and rapidly fired off 160 pictures in the first 20 minutes. The last eighty poses had nothing to do with selling the sexy sleepwear; they would be savoured in his own personal collection. Changing the lighting to a more somber and romantic tone, he emptied the last drops of "champagne" into April's glass. He watched the full effects of the alcohol in her movements now. She giggled at first when he told her to spread her legs wide, and then she flamboyantly arched her back into a pose all on her own.

"Now's the time for a new outfit," Robert said, and directed her towards the rack. "April, why don't you grab the bra and panty set and I will change my lens." This was a lie, but he knew it sounded professional. April staggered over to the rack as Robert placed the same lens back onto his Nikon.

"Do you have another bottle of champagne? I could really go for some more," she said as she pulled the tiny ensemble off of its hanger.

"Why, I sure do," Robert said, being most accommodating.

April turned around with the bra/panty set in her hand and watched the fat photographer awkwardly bend over and retrieve the second bottle out of the paper bag.

Focusing through her rapidly intoxicated vision, April supported herself on the cheap table/office desk.

"I thought you said that dog... wasn't yours?" April slightly slurred and then giggled.

"Dog?" *What the hell is this bimbo talking about?*

"I don't have a dog," he said, dismissing her. He needed to focus on standing back up.

"Really? Then who let *him* in your room?" April pointed behind Robert towards the hallway door.

As Robert stood up straight, his neck, face, and head flushed deep red from the strain. Wiping a bead of sweat from his forehead with his palm, the photographer turned around. The tenting in his pants apparent as the Viagra fully erected his penis. "What are you talking about...?"

Then Robert Pulman saw what the half-naked cheerleader was pointing at. April laughed out loud when Robert turned to look behind him; she could see the side profile of his lower section.

"Did I do that?" she giggled again.

Robert didn't answer the drunk girl. He was confused about how the black dog, (which didn't really look like a black dog up this close), got into his room? The door was locked – and still was. "How did you get in here, little fella?" he said trying to sound brave and friendly as he took a step closer.

"How do you know he was a fella? Does he have a raging hard-on too?"

"Shhh!"

As he took a step closer, Robert noticed the dog didn't move. It was completely still and silent. At this close, it looked even less like a dog. It had four legs like a dog, and a head and neck like a dog, but it had the moist, snotty snout of a bat and the eyes of a goat. However, the whites of the eyes weren't white at all, but a deep yellow like the nicotine stained fingers of a heavy smoker. It had twisted cauliflower ears on the sides of its head, and its black coat had the mossy appearance of the mould you find on blackened, rotting vegetables.

Maybe it isn't real? It can't be real. She must have put a stuffed dog there when she got changed. The bimbo is playing me.

"Are you messing with me?" he called over his shoulder.

Then it growled. The sound was more like a rattling gurgle from the back of its throat – a *grattle*. Robert stopped leaning closer. The grattle didn't sound right. It didn't sound like a cheap voice recorder that comes in a doll you win at a fair by knocking over milk bottles. No, this grattle sounded wet, and it sounded real.

Robert slowly shifted left. The creature's head and body didn't move, but its yellow goat eyes followed him. He was still partially sure the thing wasn't real, but he knew he didn't want to be this close to it either. Slowly, Robert took a step back and another wet grattle escaped from the creature.

"Well, are you going to pet it? Give it a snack. He's probably starving."

"I ain't fucking pettin' it," the photographer said, almost too softly, afraid to show fear in front of the bizarre creature.

Even though the room's air conditioner was off, cold was drifting towards him from the beast's direction. As an obese individual, Robert rarely – if ever – got cold, but the whispers of cold currents drifting his way didn't just cool the surface of his skin, but also chilled it deeply. As he'd been a predator of young women and men for years, Robert forgot what it was like to be the prey. But his dominating ego was wavering there in the hotel room. Like a school bully who'd met his match, Robert Pulman decided he didn't want to play any more today. It was time to go and leave this town.

"Oh, look at you! You look terrified of that cute little pup," April said as she walked closer to the photographer. Even in her intoxicated state, April began to sense the unnatural vibe resonating from the black *dog* as she approached them. Her giddy and innocent expression slid off her face when she bumped into the photographer as he was trying to step backwards. Now only a few feet away from the creature, April was able to get a closer and clearer look.

"You've got one ugly dog."

A new instinct began tugging at April, penetrating the alcoholic fog that was dulling her senses, as though the lost guardian angels from Sunday school past were trying to warn her.

"I told you," Robert snapped, trying to back up through April. "That's not my goddamned dog. I don't even think that *is* a dog."

The creature grattled another wet growl and then opened its bat mouth wide, displaying rows upon rows of shark-like teeth. Its nicotine eyes with their horizontal squiggled pupils jittered and shot back and forth between Robert and April. More waves of cold radiated from the mossy, black creature as its body began to vibrate – lightly, at first, like the ghostly flicker of a halogen lamp. It was so slight that

Robert mistook it for his own shivering, but then the vibrating became unmistakable as its frequency intensified into violent trembling.

It felt to Robert like the creature was sucking all the heat out of the room. Robert's peripheral vision watched as the bathroom mirror and the polished, chrome faucet began to cloud over with frost, resembling the windshield of a car in late winter.

Oh my god, what is it? Robert asked himself. But, slowly, Robert began to realize what it was. And, as the realization inched into him like the creeping frost across the mirror, the black creature spoke to him inside of his head with the voice of his ex-wife.

"(*Grattle*). How could you screw around on me? I loved you. I stood by you. You ruined my life! I hate you! I curse you, Robert Pulman! (*Grattle*)." The voice then changed to a metallic grating sound. "(*Grattle*). Robert. Robbie. Bob. You have been cursed. (G*rattle*). And not just with any curse, but you, Bob, have been cursed by a woman who was truly scorned. (*Grattle*). And you know what they say about a woman scorned? Rarely do curses get used anymore. It's too bad they have fallen out of fashion, but every once in a while we get called out. I have been watching you these last few years. Nice work, we have enjoyed the show. (*Grattle*)."

Robert, transfixed and paralyzed, stared into the creature's twisted eyes. The harsh voice continued. "We have watched how you single-handedly destroyed 51 young people and then their families. You do good work, Robert. (*Grattle*)."

"I don't know what you're talking about," Robert's inner voice fired back, quivering and full of shame.

"Robbie, (*Grattle*) your life has been documented and your file is impressive. But we are closing it. This girl is not your victim to take; she is special to us."

"This girl wasn't going to be a victim." Robert tried to lie, but he knew the creature could see right through him. "What do you mean, 'you are closing my file'?" Robert blinked several times and licked his lips as he felt the moisture around his eyes, nose, and mouth begin to dry out from some invisible arctic emission.

April too felt the cold, although she was shielded by the hefty photographer. The waves of cold, which had now engulfed the room, easily penetrated the thin fabric of the lingerie.

"Why is it so cold in here? Why is it doing that... that shaking?" April asked nervously through chattering teeth, watching her breath drift out in front of her face and down towards the creature.

"B-back up b-bitch," Robert said as frost formed across his face. "I-I'm t-too close to it."

The vacuum that was drawing the heat and moisture from the room also cleared April's intoxicated and confused mind. Thinking clearly for the first time in thirty minutes, April felt exposed. Naked. Used. Embarrassed.

With a blast of mental clarity and physical alertness, April heard her evolutionary instincts screaming at her. For the first time she saw the four-legged Being for what it really was – a demon preying on the heat, and she saw the two legged photographer still sporting an erection for what he really was – a sick and disgusting perverted man who preys on the young and naive.

April stepped backed across the room, stumbled into the desk and the chrome clothes trolley, and landed hard on the floor. Reaching over, she pulled the satin sheet off of the bed. She wanted to cover herself, not only from the penetrating ribbons of cold that had crossed the room, but also from the shame that was drowning her like a tidal wave. April crouched down into the farthest corner, clutching one of the pillows from the bed in front of her the way a small child would cling to a stuffed doll after waking up from a nightmare. Her chin still chattered from the chill – both physically and psychologically. The whole time April never blinked or said a word; she just stared at the vibrating demon and the fat asshole standing only a few feet away from it.

Frost had already built up around Robert's face. His cheeks, normally red from being flushed, were now white from frost bite. Tiny capillaries just under the surface of his skin crystallized and split, exposing more tissue that also began to freeze. It was an excruciating cycle of freezing, splitting, and freezing again.

Robert Pulman could feel the exposed skin on his face and neck freeze and crack. The moisture in his nose and sinus cavity was rapidly drying out. His lips had already passed the point of severe wind burn and he felt a crack in the centre of his bottom lip stretch and split, dividing his lip into two halves and exposing his bottom teeth to the extreme cold. Robert wanted to scream in pain and agony. He meant to scream, but his tongue had already dried and it too was freezing up. It became thick and voiceless like the leather tongue of a shoe. The soft skin on the roof of his mouth popped and crackled as the fine membrane between his throat and sinus was robbed of its moisture. He felt a hole form and heard a high-pitched hiss as the little pressure gradient between his nasal cavity and his throat equalized. As the remaining skin stretched and dried, he could feel it give away. His head filled with intense pain as the membrane split and curled into itself. Still, the dead and frozen skin seemed to stay electrified.

The unnatural vacuum that was being drawn in from the demon funneled the arctic air into Robert's nose and out of his mouth, creating a hollow hum from the vibrating of small, lacrimal bones.

Only half a minute ago he was trying to back up, bumping into that dumb little bitch, but now his face was so cold it felt like it was on fire; every exposed nerve was somehow still alive and screaming, which was something he wished he could do. He wanted to shield his face with his hands but his shoulders and arms wouldn't move, as if they were obeying their own survival instincts. He tried to blink and remoisten his freeze-dried eyes, but the thin layer of skin of his eye lids caught on the frozen cornea, leaving his eyes in a half-open sleepy expression. His lungs burned as the moisture and air was pulled out of them and waves of cold air were forced in, freezing each individual alveolus as though they were missed grapes still left on the vine in the dead of winter.

Oh my God, it's killing me. It is freezing me to death. He was unable to blink, unable to move, and unable to scream.

Rapidly freezing to death and suffocating as his lungs snapped and crackled like Rice Krispies, Robert Pulman sat front and center as pictures of his life began to play out before him.

His eyes, now frozen solid, could no longer see. The four-legged demon continued to bask in Robert's torment as it replayed his deceitful and selfish life, victim after victim. In his mind, Robert saw young men and women lied to and played with like they were cat toys being batted around from one cheap hotel room to the next.

The extreme cold that broadcasted off of the demon had already penetrated Robert's ears and ruptured the internal canals. His skin that had been protected by the dress shirt and blue jeans began to freeze and adhere to the clothing. Robert could feel the sensitive tip of his still solid erection burn from the cold. His testicles pulled themselves deep into his body for protection, but even there the cold penetrated in, guided and willed by unseen fingers.

Jesus, sweet brother Jesus, please protect me, Robert screamed inside.

The beast laughed out loud and, for the first time, spoke out into the room. "(*Grattle*). He's not here with you. There is no god (*Grattle*) here with you, Robert."

With that, the demon's four legs divided into eight, and, like a spider, its new legs spread themselves wide. The legs reached high up the wall and onto the ceiling. Its clawed paws gripped the gyprock and stucco, and its body filled the stunted hallway.

Blind, mute, deaf, and helpless, Robert stood in the Sea Side Inn, frozen but alive. He could no longer breathe, but he stood there trapped in the intense agony of his frozen body.

"How about if we get you off one last time, Robert?" his wife's voice returned in his head.

Robert felt a new searing of unprecedented torture as the demon reached out a black arm, shredded open the frozen cotton material of his jeans, and wrapped a finger-like claw around his solid penis. Robert knew that the skin, tissue, and nerve cells of his body were surely frozen and dead, but the physical touch of the beast shot pain straight through to his soul. He couldn't escape physically, as his body was immobile and solid, or into death, as his soul couldn't drift.

He awaited and longed for the thawing fires of hell that he was sure he was going to be plunged into. The demon raised itself high on its legs and looked into the now-frozen white eyes of Robert Pulman. It readjusted and slid its claw back and forth on his erection. With each movement, Robert screamed in agony deep within his frozen, plump tomb. The demon's jerking became quicker and more aggressive.

Begging for the fires of hell, Robert prayed to Satan himself to take his soul. The demon's bat-like snout smiled as he felt the human's despair, its panic, its pain.

The beast stopped its claw dead. "You want relief, Robert?" it said in his ex-wife's voice. There was humour in her tone.

Disoriented with pain, Robert's soul felt like it was plunged into the North Atlantic Ocean and was drowning in a sea of needles.

"Yes... relief... please give me relief. Take me to the depths of hell. Burn my flesh in the lakes of fire. Anything but this cold."

"Fires of hell? (*Grattle*)," the demon laughed and retightened its grip on Robert's cock. "This (*Grattle*) is your hell." Then, as the demon began to feast on Robert's frozen face, it twisted and broke off his penis.

From the far corner, April watched the dog/spider wrap its legs around the solid torso of Robert Pulman and begin devouring his face. Pieces of frozen skin, bone, and red-coloured ice chips fell to the floor as it ravaged the photographer.

When the creature was finished it looked over at the teenager crouched in the corner, hiding behind the sheets and a pillow for protection. Its eight legs nimbly walked around the room to the other side of the bed.

"April, (*Grattle*)," it said as it lowered its face to be in line with hers, "be not afraid. I cannot harm you. (*Grattle*)."

At these words from the demon, April blinked and snapped out of her fear. "What are you?" she asked, staring back into its twisted eyes.

"Family," the demon replied. "I am called Asmodeus."

A strange sensation flooded April, like the déjà vu of an old dream. She sensed some kind of familiarity with the hideous demon.

April slowly released the "death" grip she had on the pillow. Only inches away from the beast, she allowed herself to examine the outline of its head. She looked at its deformed ears, and its bat-like mouth that contained multiple rows of teeth with pieces of Robert wedged in between. She looked at the folds of its jaw, and at its elongated neck and mossy frame. Her eyes followed its eight, long, v-shaped spider-like legs.

The demon sensed her easing trepidation. It watched as the teenager reached out and caressed the side of its face. The demon could feel the warmth of the human's hand, and its blood pulsing just beneath the skins surface. It stared into the eyes of the girl, and the girl, in return, matched its gaze, her hand never leaving its face.

The door swung open and from the hallway and in stepped a tall, barefoot man with white hair and pale skin wearing a white tuxedo. He gracefully crossed the room and stood behind the creature. The demon looked back and smiled a horrific grin, and then bowed his head in reverence. The pale stranger looked down and gave April a genuine smile. He stepped closer and extended his hand to help her off the floor. The mossy demon took several side steps up the wall to make room for him.

"Who are you?" April asked, unsure about her next move.

"You can call me... father. And I have something for you. Something... donated by an old friend. He's not going to need it anymore." Lucifer pulled out a gold box from his breast pocket. It was about the same size and shape as a standard ring box. April eyed the golden case with awe. The small engravings etched into the sides of the box depicting the battle between Lucifer and Adam came to life in front of her.

She didn't believe this stranger was actually her long-lost father. Well, maybe she did – kind of. There was something very familiar about him, besides the white hair. After all, meeting her real father in a hotel room wouldn't be the strangest thing to happen to her today; the eight-legged dog-demon that ate the photographer took that prize.

"Take it. It is for you," Lucifer said, balancing the cube on his open palm.

April couldn't take her eyes off of it. It was beautiful, enticing, powerful, and unnatural – all wrapped into a sparkling, golden, two-inch square box. It pulled her into a trance. She forgot to ask common sense questions like, *Where have you been all my life? How did you find me?* and *Do I look like mom?*

They didn't seem to matter. Instead, she reached out and plucked the case from his hand. The box weighed almost nothing, but still felt very solid and durable. Instantly, the engraved pictures changed from

Lucifer's battle scene to April's own hotel scenario, complete with the devouring of Robert Pulman.

"How does it do that?" she asked, rotating the box and watching the scene from the outer four sides. The top and bottom of the box remained smooth.

"It is a *kind* of magic. A very old magic," Lucifer said, watching his young anti-Christ.

"Like ancient vampire magic?" April asked.

Lucifer smiled a warm, condescending smile.

"Older."

"What's inside of it?"

"Go ahead and open it," Lucifer urged her.

With her left hand, April lifted the thin, flat lid and cracked the case open. Inside there was a wet and glistening piece of red meat. She tilted the box and the piece slid out onto her waiting palm, staining her skin red.

"What is it? Meat?" she asked.

"It is a piece of heart," Satan said matter-of-factly.

"Heart? Ew. This is a raw piece of cow's heart?" April said, making a face of disgust. She squeezed the small morsel between her fingers, forcing tiny drops of blood to the surface. Then she stared at the small piece of flesh, rolling it around with her fingers. April thought she could still feel a faint pulse, which of course was impossible. All the same, she was drawn to its moist and spongy texture. The heart was somehow beckoning her, calling to her.

Lucifer knew she could feel its power. "Not a cow's heart, my young thing. It came from an old friend of mine. Before I threw his soul into a lake of fire, I removed his last bit of divine essence."

Asmodeus eyed the chunk of meat and Lucifer eyed the demon.

"It is for you alone, April," Lucifer said, making it clear the prize was not for anyone else. "I want you to have it. It will bring you strength and life in ways you have never known."

Lucifer smiled at the thought of ruling eternity with an heir of his own.

"Like vampires, we could live forever," April added, her eyes shining at the thought.

Lucifer hated the whole vampire craze. There was only one true Prince of Darkness, and he was it.

"Eat it, April. Consume the body, fulfill your destiny, and live forever," Satan held out his left hand to help her to her feet, "at my side as my Princess of Darkness."

April gave the piece of heart one last squeeze, and before she could talk herself out of it she popped it into her mouth. With the sensitivity of her tongue, she could now clearly feel the pulsing rhythm from the cubed flesh: *Thump-thump. Thump-thump.*

With each beat, April grew bolder, more confident, and more in tune to the world around her, both the natural and supernatural.

Her father standing in front of her was cascaded in shimmering, radiant light; his white wings were open and full behind him. The black dog-demon, Asmodeus, climbed down off the wall, and appeared now as a short, black man standing up to Lucifer's waist. He retained his demon face, and had four arms. In each of his hands held a small, curved, demonic sword. He wore black leather chest armour and a black Roman subligaculum (groin wrap). He smiled a razor smile and reverently bowed low, looking at the floor.

April accepted her father's hand and stood up. The pulsing morsel was slowly dissolving in her mouth, but she now felt her own heart's rhythm changing to keep time with it. As the piece continued to melt, she grew stronger. Her senses were electric. She could hear the waves crashing on the shore. Further out she could feel the wind caressing the feathers of an Osprey circling hundreds of meters above the coastline. She sensed wandering souls outside the Inn, lost in their own purgatory. She could even feel the agony coming off Robert Pulman's tormented ghost.

The more she felt, the less she cared. And the less she cared, the stronger she felt.

"Now what?" April asked, standing at his side.

"Now we go home and plan out the next 2000 years. It's my turn."

www.ingramcontent.com/pod-product-compliance
Lightning Source LLC
Chambersburg PA
CBHW060926180626
46817CB00004B/1413

* 9 7 8 0 9 9 1 7 9 2 2 0 7 *